the CURSE of EELGRASS BOG

the CURSE of EELGRASS BOG

MARY AVERLING

RAZORBILL

An imprint of Penguin Random House LLC, New York

First published in the United States of America by Razorbill,
an imprint of Penguin Random House LLC, 2024

Visit us online at PenguinRandomHouse.com.

Library of Congress Cataloging-in-Publication Data is available.

ISBN 9780593624906

Printed in the United States of America

1st Printing

LSCH

Design by Alex Campbell
Text set in Yana

To Mum,
for encouraging me to dream
from the very beginning.

1

I sneak back into the Unnatural History Museum at exactly two minutes past midnight, carrying a backpack full of bones. No one sees me. The town is half-drowned in fog, the ghostly kind that often creeps inward from Eelgrass Bog, and the watch fires burn low. Even the moon is hidden. I squeeze through a gap in the museum's hedge, only stopping when my hair snags on a branch.

Kess, a voice hisses from my backpack. *Keep moving!*

"One second." I yank my hair free. The hedge is getting wilder and meaner by the day. I need to trim it down before it swallows the footpath entirely.

Are we home now?

"Yes," I say, "so please hush up."

The Unnatural History Museum looms in front of me, a tumbledown mess of clapboard and twisted chimneys. Most windows have been covered by ivy, and on windy nights like tonight, I can hear the wood groan. It's as alive as a building can be—for now. I have a pretty good nose for sniffing out dead things, better than most people, and I can smell the rot in the walls.

The voice in my backpack coughs loudly.

"Yes, yes," I grumble. "Be patient."

The front doors are too noisy to use, despite how frequently I've oiled them. They've had rusted hinges for as long as I can remember, and the doorknobs hang like loose teeth. But this is my home. I know every mouse crack and hidden entrance, including where ivy grows overtop an unlocked window.

I wrench up the sash and roll inside with a flurry of dead leaves. Once the window is shut again, I adjust my round-rimmed glasses and scan the gloom in case Oliver is awake and waiting to ambush me. Somewhere a leaky pipe goes *drip, drip*. Aside from a couple of spiders scuttling across display cases, everyone—and everything—seems to be asleep. Good. I take a big, relieved breath and instantly regret it.

"It reeks in here," I say.

Obviously. That would be me.

I wrinkle my nose. "It's worse than you."

Oh. The voice sounds disappointed. *Guess I have competition.*

I tiptoe through the main hall, and my rubber boots creak against the floorboards. I don't need a lantern. I know exactly where every exhibit is, even in the darkest dark. A chandelier hangs above my head, dripping strings of knucklebones, and behind me, dried kraken tentacles crisscross the wall like Christmas tinsel. I pass mandrakes, tusks, fossils spat from the deepest dredges of Eelgrass Bog. All dust choked and lifeless.

Up a staircase. Underneath a woolly whale skeleton that swims through the air on invisible wires. Around the bog

2

mummy exhibit, because bog mummies are too creepy in the dark even for me. Along the third-floor hallway until I find a broom closet. Once I'm safely inside, door locked and candle lit, I sit on an overturned mop bucket and pull three things from my backpack:

A pair of magnification goggles.

A paper bag full of bones.

A pickled head floating in an oversize mason jar.

Finally, the head says. *I was getting dizzy.*

Even in an unnatural history museum full of peculiar things, Shrunken Jim is real ugly. Bulbous eyes, warts, and skin the same greenish color as pond water. I know dead things shouldn't talk—especially not dead things who've had their mouths sewn shut for three hundred years—but "should" and "shouldn't" often get mixed up in Wick's End. Ever since my parents found him on Eelgrass Bog years ago, he's become kind of like my best friend.

Go on, Shrunken Jim says eagerly. *Look at the bones! Tonight's the night—I can feel it.*

"I think so too," I say. And I really mean it. Stormy nights always turn up the best bones, and I went closer to Eelgrass Bog than I usually dare. Not quite past the watch fires, but still.

What about that long one? Shrunken Jim says.

I slip the goggles overtop my regular glasses and thumb through dials until the bones come into sharp focus.

"Hmm. It's from a wing."

Ooh, perhaps it's a dragon! Or a vampire bat!

"Vampire bats are natural, silly," I say, running my fingers along the wing bone. It's a bit bendy, like a stiff shoelace. I squint extra hard and try to remember Mam's teachings. She taught me all there is to know about bones, natural and unnatural, but I have the worst memory in Wick's End. Sometimes it feels as though her lessons are moths that fly away through my ears at night.

So, I have to focus. Focus. Focus.

Carefully, I arrange the bones into a shape. Snarl-toothed skull, pebbly vertebrae, ribs, and femurs, until a skeletal creature starts to form on the floorboards.

Oh dear. Shrunken Jim's mouth-stitches turn downward. *That looks like . . .*

"A badger," I finish, sitting up on the mop bucket. "A common badger."

What about the wing?

"Hawk, probably. Not from the same animal." I tug off the goggles and wipe my watery eyes with my sleeve. "I—I was so sure."

Next time, says Shrunken Jim gently.

A draft blows through, and the walls sag. I want to smile to show that I agree, except the Unnatural History Museum doesn't have many "next times" left. No matter how grand it once was, no matter how much I love it, the museum is close to curling up and falling apart. It's lonely. It needs *people.* Ever since my parents left on their research trip to Antarctica and put my brother, Oliver, in charge, we've been collecting plenty of dust and cobwebs and rot, but absolutely zero visitors. We desperately need to bring people back. We need something *new*.

Something like an undiscovered monster, dug fresh from Eelgrass Bog.

"We'll try again tomorrow," I say. "We need to give the storm time to churn up new bones, is all."

Exactly, Shrunken Jim says, and I think he's trying to sound confident too. *I bet a truly abnormal creature is floating closer to Wick's End as we speak. Big as a house, eighteen legs, purple bones—*

A sudden *thud* cuts him off. We both go still.

"Hear that?" I whisper. A chill scuttles down my spine like a cold finger. Branches have been pounding the windows all night, but that noise came from *inside* the museum.

Sounded like a door slamming, Shrunken Jim whispers. *Is Awful Ollie awake?*

"Oh, vermin," I curse. Quickly, I cover the badger skeleton and Shrunken Jim with my coat, blow out the candle, and peer into the hallway. It's dark enough to swallow fireflies whole.

What are you doing? Shrunken Jim hisses. *Hide!*

"Hush," I whisper. "It's okay, I think it was—"

"Are you talking to your pet goblin again?"

I shriek and accidentally slam the closet door on my toes, which makes me shriek a second time. "Gah! Don't sneak up on me like that!"

Oliver strikes a match, and light washes down the hallway. His eyes are baggy and angry behind his own wire-framed glasses. We used to look alike, according to just about everyone,

5

except now he's thinner than a rake and never smiles and forgets to wash his clothes. He reeks of compost, all mildewy and bitter like a dead thing forced back to life.

"It's after midnight, Kester," he says, as if I don't know how to tell the time. "Why are you awake?"

"Um. I wanted a glass of milk."

"From the broom closet?"

"I–I got lost. It's dark."

"No candle?"

"You know me, Ollie." I shrug as carelessly as I can. "Always unprepared."

His mouth pinches. "Don't call me Ollie."

"Don't call me Kester."

We glare at each other. Oliver is fifteen, barely three years older than me, but he acts like he's the most sensible grown-up who ever existed. We used to get along, mostly. We'd put on puppet shows, catalog snails, and watch storms from the museum rooftop. Once, we bicycled to a traveling fairground together, and he bought a whole bag of caramel corn for us to share. Then Mam and Da left, and he's been a sour-faced toad ever since.

"Unprepared," he echoes. "But you remembered to bring your jacket, backpack, and goggles? To get milk?"

I scramble for an excuse. "Maybe I just– Hey!"

Oliver pushes past me and moves my jacket with the tip of his bare toe. Shrunken Jim winces. The badger skull rolls out into the hallway, stopping at my feet.

"Oops," I say.

Oliver whirls on me, furious. "Where did you get these?"

I think about lying, but he already knows the answer, so I jut out my chin and say, "Eelgrass Bog."

The museum's pipes tremble. Oliver's mouth pinches even tighter.

"How many times do we have to talk about this?" he snaps. "Strange things live on that bog, Kester, and not the sort of strange that fits into a museum. The mud will gobble the meat from your bones, and the witches—"

"Witches?" I say too eagerly.

"*Demons.* Remember, the watch fires are there for a reason. Go too far and you'll be eaten alive. And *you*"—he glares at Shrunken Jim—"should know the dangers better than anyone."

Shrunken Jim sticks his shriveled tongue through his mouth-stitches.

If Oliver is trying to scare me, he isn't doing a very good job. I've heard all these stories and worse since I was old enough to remember. But Eelgrass Bog is where the bones are, and the nastier the monster I find, the better. Nobody comes to the Unnatural History Museum to see *ordinary*.

I cross my arms. "I didn't go past the watch fires."

"Sometimes the edge is all it takes." Oliver waves his candlestick at the bones. "Get rid of these. And if you even think about visiting Eelgrass Bog again, I'll—I'll put a lock on your bedroom door."

Go ahead, I want to snap. When Mam and Da come back,

he can explain why I'm locked up and the Unnatural History Museum has gone rotten. Actually, there are lots of things I want to say to Oliver. I want to show him how loudly the walls are groaning, the cracks and too-thick ivy, the loneliness stitched up in every floorboard. I want him to notice how the exhibits are choking in dust because nobody else cares enough to clean them. I want him to realize how disappointed Mam and Da will be when they return.

Once, maybe I could've spoken to him properly. But there's no point anymore. He won't listen to me. No one ever does. I could be a wood louse, for all the difference I manage to make around here.

"Okay," I say, hating how small my voice sounds.

He pushes up his glasses. "Good night, Kester."

"Night, Ollie."

I watch him go. My heart hollow-beats. Then I collect the bones into my backpack, grab Shrunken Jim's jar, and tiptoe out of the closet into the dark.

2

I sleep for longer than usual. Ordinarily, I'm up at the crack of dawn to begin my chores, but I've been extra tired since summer ended. My dreams are full of flowers, of petals in impossibly bright colors and how it might feel to run barefoot through a garden. Not a prickly garden like we've got out front. I dream of the kind Mam used to grow, with lush green grass and blossoms, though I can't remember if she kept roses or tulips. There's nothing left but weeds now.

I slip out of bed and pull on knitted socks. The fog is thick as butter outside. I can barely see the wooden spines of our neighbors' rooftops.

Look who's alive, Shrunken Jim says from his perch on my windowsill. *Good dreams?*

"The best." I put on my glasses, tug my fingers through my short brown hair, and fetch an envelope marked STOWELL BASE, ANTARCTICA from my desk. "Be right back."

The Unnatural History Museum is waking up too. As I shuffle downstairs, wincing at my sleep-stiff bones, pipes clank, and walls appear to shiver in the drafts. I try to greet as many exhibits as I can. Shrunken Jim might be the only unnatural thing in the museum that talks, but sometimes it feels like the preserved specimens in jars and cabinets are listening too. I guess it helps everything feel less empty, like I'm a little less alone.

The kitchen is the ugliest room in the whole museum. That's a fact, not just my opinion. It's a stale, used-tissue sort of old, with peeling yellow cabinets and an ancient fridge that always wails like a startled chicken. My parents aren't cooks, and Oliver *especially* isn't. I can't remember the last time he set foot in the kitchen or a grocery store. I poke through the cupboards and find nothing but pickled cockles, black bread, and a box of crackers that looks older than me.

"Cockle sandwich it is," I mutter.

I make two. I start chewing one right away (vinegary but not too bad), and the other I put on a chipped plate and bring to Oliver. On my way, I pick up a copy of the *Wick's End Daily* from the front doorway. Pages are scattered over the steps, like someone threw it and ran away in a hurry—as usual.

"Ollie!" I bang on the library door. "Breakfast!"

"Go away!"

"I have your newspaper."

The door clicks open. Oliver hasn't bothered to comb his hair, and ink is smudged over his skinny forearms. He looks as though he belongs inside a museum cabinet, the type of exhibit that collects dust in the basement because it's too shabby for display. He scowls at the sandwich. "Whatever that is, it needs to be burned, not eaten."

"How can you tell it's bad if you haven't tried it?"

"There's mold on the bread," Oliver says. He reaches for the newspaper, but I step back.

"Nope," I say. "You have to promise to eat breakfast if you want the newspaper. Package deal."

Oliver's lips thin until they're practically sewn together like Shrunken Jim's. "You aren't Mam, Kester. They left *me* in charge, not you."

"Maybe you should make your own sandwiches, then."

"I'm too busy working."

"On what?"

"You know what," he says. "Paperwork. Same as yesterday, and the day before that, and the day before that."

I scoff. "Mam and Da never spent all day with paperwork."

"Perhaps you didn't pay attention. Not everyone gets to play around digging up rat bones," he says bitterly. "Running a museum takes practical stuff too. Ledgers, catalogs, lists. You wouldn't understand."

"I would if you explained it better."

Oliver just glowers. "Give me the newspaper, and I'll eat your moldy abomination. Then go away."

I hand everything over. "For the record, I'm digging up *monster* bones. It's not *play*. Also, can I have a stamp for my letter? I want to ask Mam and Da when they're coming home and—"

"I'll mail it," Oliver interrupts. He snatches the letter from under my arm and stuffs it into his pocket.

"Fine. Just make sure you mail it soon, and also try to eat your *whole* breakfast, because Mam said—"

The door slams in my face.

I curl my toes. I really don't know why I bother. I should let Oliver waste away doing whatever more-important-than-the-rest-of-the-world stuff he does in the library all day. It can't actually be work. Otherwise he'd have something to show for it. I reckon he just enjoys sitting in the library like my parents always did, pretending to be scholarly and important, pretending to be grown-up. It's annoying because my parents never locked the library–Da let me sit on his lap with my favorite atlas, the one with sea beasts lurking in the corners, and Mam let me help organize bookshelves in whatever order I wanted. *Libraries aren't tombs*, they'd say. *No need to keep them quiet and dusty.* Sure, I prefer bones to books, but my throat turns itchy if I think too hard about how things have changed since they left. Sometimes, I secretly wish Oliver had left instead of my parents.

But Mam told me to take care of the museum, and that means Oliver too. Especially because he isn't very good at taking care of himself.

How was Mr. Misery this morning? Shrunken Jim asks when I return to my room. *The Most Petulant Pedrock? Our Cantankerous King?*

"Cantankerous," I say. "That's a good word."

Shrunken Jim smiles through his mouth-stitches. *Obdurate is a good one too. It means "pigheaded."*

I get dressed in my favorite red cardigan and Da's old mustard waistcoat, muttering "obdurate" to myself as I fumble with the buttons. It isn't a weekend, which means I'm supposed to spend the day reading schoolbooks. However, textbook facts never stick in my cobweb-brain very well, and I've got more important business today than trying to learn far-off capital cities or how to properly measure a triangle.

So instead, I go back to the broom closet. This time I take an actual broom.

Shrunken Jim fits into the special mesh pocket I made just for him on the outside of my backpack. We choose the loudest record from Mam's music collection, a soaring, drum-heavy symphony, and put it on full blast so the whole building vibrates. It's perfect. Even if Oliver yells at me to turn it off, I won't be able to hear him.

Sometimes I almost enjoy cleaning days, especially when the music is loud enough to drown out gloomy thoughts. I dance around the museum, knocking down cobwebs, polishing display cases, and singing with Shrunken Jim at the top of my lungs. My parents always encouraged loudness. *Plenty of time for silence when you're dead*, they'd say, even though Shrunken Jim can sing pretty well too. It makes me wonder if they have music at their research base in Antarctica. Maybe I'll send a couple of records with my next letter, just in case.

I sweep, scrub, and chase away hordes of silverfish and spiders. I polish the plaques on display cases, especially the ones that have my parents' names: DISCOVERED BY DR. ELLEN-JANE PEDROCK or CATALOGED BY DR. HUGH PEDROCK. It's incredible how much stuff in the museum was found directly by them. It does make me feel a bit useless since I can't seem to find more than a couple of badger bones. But that's the kind of gloomy thought I want to banish. I turn the record player louder, singing until my throat hurts. For a while, it feels like I really have brought the Unnatural History Museum back to life. The woolly whale skeleton seems to dance on the ceiling, bog mummies bask in the weak morning sunlight, and even the doorknobs seem less rusty. I paste wallpaper back onto walls. Scrub mold from the second-floor bathroom. Clear ash from all six fireplaces. Re-arrange bone dolls in the Hall of Curses exhibit. Water mandrakes. Brush dragon teeth.

Not bad, Shrunken Jim says when we take a break. *If your parents walked through the doors right this minute, I don't think they could find a hair out of place.*

"Liar." I tie my hair into a ponytail. My head is pounding from the music, and my palms have blistered. But that's part of the job. Someone has to act alive around here, or else the museum might forget what "alive" means.

Shrunken Jim bobs in his jar. *You do them proud.*

I grin tiredly and lean against a tank of preserved flesh-eating seaweed. He's being sweet, but he really is a fibber. No matter how hard I work to polish its surface, the Unnatural History Museum is crumbling in places I can't seem to reach. I can dust exhibits, but I can't stop them from growing brittle and rotten and mildewy. I can't chase away *all* the spiders. I can't catch *all* the moth eggs. Not by myself. Perhaps if I wasn't rattling around in here like a pea in a whistle, I might be able to make a real difference. But caring for the Unnatural History Museum by myself is like trying to fill a bucket with a hole in the bottom.

There are photographs lining the walls from before Mam and Da left. Things were different then. Everything, from the staircases to the display cabinets, shone with care. The pests were always under control. The wallpaper wasn't peeling and mold spotted. People came from across the country to visit us, bringing ticket money that helped the museum thrive. I try and try and try, but I'm missing the kind of magic Mam and Da had. They never needed to work so hard to keep the museum from crumbling away.

It's unfortunate that I lost my body, Shrunken Jim sighs. *Otherwise I could help.*

I shift upright. "Tell me that story again?"

I've told you a thousand times, Kess.

"Ages ago. I barely remember the details," I say, blowing a stream of dust from the seaweed tank. It swirls like a galaxy. "Tell me again, please? And don't leave the nasty parts out."

Shrunken Jim sighs louder, though I reckon he loves talking about himself. His voice always goes wistful whenever he mentions Eelgrass Bog, no matter how he insists it's full of danger and darkness. My favorite tales are about his adventures in the Drowned World, which is exactly where today's tale takes place.

The Drowned World is a secret place beneath the bog, so deep underground, it has its own impossible stars. It's a place full of creatures so ancient there aren't human words to describe them, with a river brimming with pure gold. Shrunken Jim says this is the source of all the unnatural magic on Eelgrass Bog. He also says he was kicked out and stuffed into a jar by a witch who was jealous of his beauty, so it's tricky to know how much he's telling the truth. But it doesn't matter. Real or unreal, hearing about Eelgrass Bog is like settling into a favorite armchair. Soon I feel wistful too, even though *I'll* probably never visit. But that's what the best stories do. They let you see yourself perfectly, all your dreams and complicated parts you can't otherwise put your finger on, as though the words know you better than you know yourself. Even now, I don't really understand why stories about Eelgrass Bog feel so right. They just do. It must be like how science feels to my parents. Like maybe we aren't so alone after all.

Hey, it's not bedtime yet, Shrunken Jim says. *Are you falling asleep on me? Am I that dull?*

"Course not," I yawn.

Uh-huh. You've got drool on your chin.

I wipe it off. "Guess it's lunchtime. Hungry?"

Excuses, excuses, Shrunken Jim grumbles. But his mouth-stitches are tugged upward.

My body is extra stiff after lying down for so long. When I stand, I knock a fresh cobweb from the seaweed tank. It falls slowly through a sunbeam before coming to rest on the floorboards, where a spider is scuttling out of view.

Lunch is another cockle sandwich. I choke it down, then fetch clippers from our very, very tumbledown shed and start on the hedgerow. The fog has finally started to burn off. A hawk soars overhead. I watch it circle and imagine sprouting wings of my own. I'd fly over the watch fires to Shrunken Jim's Drowned World, find monster skeletons, and bring them home with daylight to spare.

Focus, Kess, Shrunken Jim says gently.

"Right," I say. Daydreaming probably isn't sensible when I'm holding gigantic gardening scissors.

I chop tangled branches until the footpath is bare again. Ivy has knotted itself into the boxwoods, so I cut that away too. All the while, Shrunken Jim and I hum the same song, one that my parents used to dance to when they thought Oliver and I were in bed: *Take my hand, oh my darling; we'll outrun the dark. Don't go away now; you have stolen my heart.* Oliver would hold a finger to his lips, and we'd spin in dizzy circles on the landing until I laughed too loud and Da shouted for us to go back to bed.

Now those days seem longer ago and more impossible than Shrunken Jim's stories.

Hey, Kess? Shrunken Jim says. *We have company.*

"Company?" I say, confused.

Then I notice the girl. My clippers freeze mid-clip.

Instead of walking on by, the girl has stopped in front of the Unnatural History Museum's gate. She looks about my age, dressed in a gray wool coat and brown leather boots. Her hair, black as a rook's wings, is neatly parted into two braids, one a little longer than the other.

She frowns. Just when I think she's going to leave, she steps through the gate and opens the front doors.

The hinges screech in surprise. Or maybe that's just me.

"Did she just . . . ?" I stammer.

Indeed, Shrunken Jim says, froggish eyes widening. *I believe we have a visitor.*

3

A visitor? A visitor! For a startled moment I just hold my clippers open. Whenever I imagine people returning to the Unnatural History Museum, it's always with crowds and fanfare. Maybe a parade or two. Not a girl quietly coming on her own.

But it doesn't matter. We have a visitor!

What are you waiting for? Shrunken Jim prods. *Go and introduce yourself.*

"Right," I say, quickly tossing down the clippers. My shoelaces have untied, and I stumble over the threshold like some kind of clumsy mermaid. "Hello?"

The girl turns away from a bog-unicorn exhibit and smiles. Her teeth are silvered by metal wires. "Ah, good, you're open! Elliott said this place was cursed or haunted or something, so I wondered—" She catches herself. "Sorry. Didn't mean it like that. Of course there are no such things as curses! Guess I'm just excited. We didn't have an unnatural history museum in Ontario."

I blink. She sounds as though she swallowed up a song from somewhere distant, every word quick and musical. It's pretty.

It's also the most anybody has spoken to me in ages, except for Oliver and Shrunken Jim. Suddenly my shirt feels very tight.

I cough the dust from my throat and mumble, "I'm Kess Pedrock."

"Lilou," she says. "Lilou Starling."

"That's a nice name."

Her smile widens. "How much does it cost to go inside? Do I need to buy a ticket from you?"

Tell her it's a hundred dollars, Shrunken Jim whispers from my backpack. *No! Two hundred! Think of how many pickles you could buy.*

But that's the problem. I can't think very well. My darned cobweb-brain barely remembers what I'm supposed to do when a visitor comes. I used to run the cash register when my parents were busy, but I can't remember how much tickets cost. The register itself hasn't worked in ages, stiffened up like a rusted spring. For some reason, the longer I look at Lilou, the sludgier my brain becomes—but it's a pleasant kind of sludgy, like melted Popsicles in the summertime.

Focus, Kess, I think. *Focus.*

"Two dollars?" I guess. That's about what a couple of chocolate bars cost. Seems fair.

Lilou counts out a handful of coins. "My birthday party was last week, so I have plenty of pocket money from my grandparents. I would've invited you if I'd known you existed. All my real friends are in Ontario, see, except—" She cuts off again, sheepish. "Sorry. You won't care about that."

I nod, although I'm sure I would care. She gives me the final coin, and it's still warm from her pocket.

Rip-off, Shrunken Jim mutters.

"Would you like a guide?" I ask, tearing off a faded UHM ticket from a roll and handing it to her.

"No thank you. I'll manage." Lilou's deep brown eyes linger on me for a second longer. Searching. Then she goes off toward the kraken tentacles, and I'm left with a stack of coins and a strange double-skip in my heart.

I would've invited you if I'd known you existed. I repeat the words over and over until they nestle somewhere deep in my rib cage, sunshine warm, filling a space I hadn't realized was empty before.

Lilou said she wants to explore alone. But I can't help worrying that if I let her go, she'll fall through a rotten floorboard or something. So, I creep behind her as she walks through different rooms and frowns at the exhibits like they're a puzzle she wants to solve. Sometimes she takes a small, flat device from her pocket and clicks what I think is a photo. Whenever she turns around, I duck behind a display case.

Why don't you go talk to her? Shrunken Jim sighs. *Skulls and vermin, Kess. I doubt she bites.*

"I did talk to her," I say, carefully avoiding a taxidermy fish with a missing glass eye. "Anyway, I don't want to scare her off."

Acting like a ghost might do the trick.

"Oh hush."

My parents were great with strangers. Da could remember

the names of everyone in Wick's End, and Mam knew how to coax a laugh from the sternest schoolteacher. Even Oliver used to make friends wherever he went, before he decided to become a prune-hearted cockroach. It's not that I'm *shy* or anything. But sometimes it feels as though I'm watching the world from behind display glass, like maybe I'm missing the half of me that understands other people. That's probably why Shrunken Jim is my best friend. I never know how to act with real humans. Lilou is the first kid my age who I've spoken to in forever—I can't mess it up.

Anyway, there's a lot you can tell about someone who doesn't know they're being watched, same as you can drag stories from bones. Example: Lilou seems to be hunting for something. Her eyes scan every inch of the museum. She passes through entire exhibits without pause, then takes pictures of a framed Eelgrass Bog map from about a thousand different angles.

"What's she looking for?" I whisper, craning my neck around a door frame.

A place to hide from you?

I flick Shrunken Jim's jar. "Nope. Look, now she's photographing another map! Can she even read Latin?"

Nefarious, I'm sure.

"Nefarious," I echo. "Nice word."

Lilou skips the Skeleton Gallery—I'm almost offended—then frowns at the Hall of Curses for half an hour. Sometimes she scribbles in a pink spiral notebook. Mostly she takes pictures. Her face stays focused and serious. I wait until she moves

onward to the Bog Mummy Room, then tiptoe after her. Well.
I *try* to tiptoe, but the floorboards creak when I step on them.

Lilou turns warily. "Hello? Kess?"

That's you, by the way, Shrunken Jim says.

"Shut up," I whisper.

Luckily there are enough rumbles and hisses in the Unnatural History Museum to cover for me. Lilou soon turns her attention to the Bowing Lion. It's some kind of ancient megacat that got preserved in the peat of Eelgrass Bog, forever frozen in a twisted position like it's bowing to a queen nobody else can see. Lilou raises her device. I gather my bravery.

"Ah, yes," I say in my best museum-expert voice, sauntering into the room like I just so happened to be passing through. "The Bowing Lion. Almost ten thousand years old, that. Do you like mummies?"

Lilou hastily stuffs her device into her pocket. "Oh! Um, I–I guess so."

I wait for her to say something else. "Bet you never had one of these in Omtrio."

"Ontario."

"Exactly."

Lilou gives me a side-eye, like she's waiting for me to pick up the hint and leave. I probably should. But then I might regret it forever. The warm, sludgy feeling makes my heart quick-beat, and I realize that I desperately don't want Lilou to think I'm weird or cursed. I want her to like me.

Thankfully, Lilou seems to give up on waiting for me to

leave. She crouches and looks at the plaque beneath the display glass. "'Leo lustrum major, female. Discovered by Drs. Ellen-Jane and Hugh Pedrock, Eelgrass Bog,'" she reads. "Are you related?"

"They're my parents," I say proudly.

"How come the dates are scratched out?"

"Um, not sure," I admit. "Probably an accident."

"Can I touch it?"

I blink in surprise. "Oh. Um. Sure."

Lilou reaches over the glass and carefully strokes two fingers along the Bowing Lion's matted mane. She doesn't seem disgusted like some people are when they touch dead things. More thoughtful. Bog mummies always make me thoughtful too, about what the mud takes and what it leaves behind. After ten thousand years, there's so much we don't understand about the Bowing Lion. But if you know where to look, parts of her story are written across her body. In her teeth and bones and skin.

"It's actually real." Lilou sounds impressed. "My dads warned me this museum was probably full of fakes, but it's actually real!"

Her dads sound like wet socks, Shrunken Jim says.

"My mam thinks whole-wheat bread tastes the same as chocolate croissants," I say. "You can't always trust parents."

Lilou cracks a smile. "Suppose not. But like . . . you also have kraken tentacles literally everywhere."

"Of course," I say more defensively. "We have lots of old megafauna in the museum, and they're *all* real."

"Megafauna?"

"Giant animals. Most natural megafauna went extinct after

24

the last ice age, but my parents found our museum specimens on Eelgrass Bog—which is really special. Usually they only surface in faraway frozen places, so the bog . . ." I clear my throat. "Anyway. We don't keep fakes."

"Of course, I'm sorry." Lilou pulls her hand out of the display case. "I didn't mean to sound rude." She pauses. "Where *are* your parents, by the way?"

"They're in Antarctica," I explain. "There's an island where ice caps have melted and weird skeletons keep appearing, so they were asked to investigate."

"They sound cool." Lilou pulls a face. "My dads are real estate agents. Have yours been gone long?"

My cobweb-brain jumps like a scratched record. A month? Three months? How long does it take for a garden to become overgrown? A needling ache stabs through my temple, and I blurt, "A while. It's not so bad. I hate cleaning bathrooms by myself, but it could be a lot worse."

"You're here *alone*?"

"Well, I have my brother, but he's a lazy turnip weevil. Shrunken Jim is my main friend," I say, gesturing. Too late, I realize it might be a little weird to call a pickled head my main friend.

Sure enough, Lilou's eyebrows almost disappear into her hairline. Her arms fold, same as Mam's whenever I tell an outrageous lie. "That's . . . that's a head in a jar, Kess."

"He talks," I say hastily. But that only makes her eyebrows climb higher.

Pleasure to meet you, Shrunken Jim says.

Lilou doesn't answer. I can't tell if she didn't hear him, or if she's just too startled for words.

I stuff my fists in my pocket so she won't see how clammy they're getting. "You took lots of photographs," I say to change the subject. "Are you looking for anything in particular?"

Somehow that makes everything worse. Walls fly up behind Lilou's eyes. "Not really," she says in the same too-casual voice. "Guess I'm just interested in Eelgrass Bog. We have to do a project about it at school."

"Ah?"

"Mm."

Lilou scuffs her boots. She's either got a secret, or I've said something wrong. I wonder if it'd help if I told some of my favorite Eelgrass Bog tales, the ones with lung-thieving shadows and predator puddles. But the air has changed. She isn't smiling anymore, and I wish I could wind back time to start this conversation from scratch.

"I should go," she says. "I'll get in trouble if I'm not home for dinner. I said I was studying at Elliott's."

"Are you sure?" I say desperately. "I could . . . I could show you the bone dolls? I just dusted them this morning. Or on the second floor, there's a glowing fossil that—"

"Sorry, Kess." She checks the screen of her device. "I'll come back if I've missed something from my gra—um, for the project."

There's nothing I can do. Lilou hurries downstairs and out the front doors. Not once does she look back. I hear the door slam, and then everything goes too quiet. I am alone again.

26

My throat squeezes. "Why do I have to be such a gullet-blabber, Jim?"

Pfft. She was the gullet-blabber, he says. *Just because I lack certain appendages, doesn't mean I can't be a superior best friend.*

"She'll tell everyone I'm strange. Then people will stay away from the museum even more." I sigh and slide down a wall until I'm lying on the floor. "What if she never comes back?"

Good riddance.

"But she was hiding something too," I say, because if that's true, maybe I'm not the only reason she wanted to leave. Maybe she was protecting something.

Shrunken Jim scoffs. *So?*

"So, I want to know what her secrets are."

A prissy sense-spouter like her? Shrunken Jim rolls his eyeballs. *If she has secrets, I bet they're dull. She probably cheats on crossword puzzles, or feeds her hamster leftover spinach.*

"Forget it," I say glumly. I'm too heart-dark for arguments right now. Anyway, the more I think about it, the more mysterious Lilou becomes. Why did she lie to her parents if she was visiting for a school project? Why come alone, if she's friends with this Elliott-whoever?

And why did she freeze up when I asked what she was searching for?

4

The Unnatural History Museum seems a little brighter after Lilou's visit, a little less lonely. Sure, the building is still choking with cobwebs and rot and mold. But somehow those problems don't seem as bad as usual. We've had a *visitor*. Even if the circumstances were strange, Lilou was still *here*. For the first time in ages, I'll have proper good news to tell Mam and Da.

I sit down at my desk and spit into a pot of dried-up ink. After I stir it with my pinkie, the ink turns sludgy enough for me to dip my hawk-feather quill and start writing.

Dear Mam & Da, I scratch out. *How's the weather in Antarctica?*

Shrunken Jim peers at the letter and snorts. *Cold, I expect.*

"It's polite to ask," I say. But I scribble over the line and start again.

Dear Mam & Da. I hope you are okay. We had a new visitor today, a girl who moved here from Ontario. Her name is Lilou Starling and she's my age and she invited me to her birthday party—

Shrunken Jim rolls his eyes. *Sure she did, Kess.*

This time I don't cross it out. "It counts," I say. "Hush up or I'll pour ink into your jar."

—which is very nice. Perhaps she'll bring her new school friends to the museum too, and we'll—

Clunk. The leg of my desk snaps clean in half, spilling my ink pot and making my quill cut a long wobbly line across the page. Shrunken Jim's jar teeters, but I catch him just before he falls.

"Wood rot," I say wearily, checking the broken leg. "Guess I need a new desk, huh?"

I'll say, Shrunken Jim huffs. *Is your letter okay?*

Luckily the ink wasn't runny enough to seep into my paper. I could just about scoop it back into the pot. Before I can try, I notice that one of my framed photographs has toppled over on a nearby shelf.

It's an old, grainy one of me, Oliver, Mam, and Da on a trip to the seaside. Maine, I think, though I can't remember for sure. We're smiling and holding triple-scooped ice creams like swords, our brown hair wind pulled and specked with pale sand. A few seconds after the picture was taken, Oliver stole a lick of my ice cream, and I threw a crab at him. Da tried to tell us to stop, but our glasses were wonky and there was melted ice cream everywhere and none of us could stop laughing.

Now there's a crack right down the middle of the glass.

"It's okay," I say, even though Shrunken Jim hasn't spoken. "It's stuff that can be fixed."

Shrunken Jim knits his eyebrow-stitches together, as though he wants to say something but isn't sure how.

I put the broken picture back on the shelf, fold my unfinished letter, and prop up the desk with a stack of Oliver's dullest schoolbooks. If I squint, nothing looks different at all.

The next morning, I slip the letter under Oliver's door with his newspaper and a note that says *Please mail soon.* It's all he's getting for breakfast today. The bread has gone rock-solid, and there's stuff floating in the vinegar that definitely isn't cockles.

Reluctantly, I button up my thickest yellow cardigan, plop Shrunken Jim into my backpack, and gather up the money from Lilou's visit alongside a handful of bills from our almost empty FOR GROCERIES jar. I suspect Oliver steals from the jar sometimes, because it used to be full, and I can't remember spending so much of it. But that's an argument for another day. Right now I'm too resigned—I *hate* grocery chores. It means I have to visit Wick's End in the daytime, when it's full of people and cars and all the wrong kinds of noises. I always feel out of my depth, like the whole town shares a secret I've never been able to understand. Still, food is important. As much as I enjoy finding skeletons, I don't fancy becoming one.

The clouds are low, like the sky has sunk into Wick's End, and it's drizzling. People scuttle around with their hoods pulled up. Great clanking trucks leave oily skins on top of puddles. Streetlamps buzz drearily. I hum to myself to block out the bleakness and the clamor: *Take my hand, oh my darling; we'll outrun the dark . . .*

By the time I get to Wick's End Convenience, my glasses are fogged and my already bushy hair has frizzed even more. A bell ding-dings when I stumble inside. It must be too miserable for shopping today, because there's no one else around—just me, aisles of teetering shelves, and awful electric lights that make my eyes hurt.

"Close the door, would you? It's freezing."

I pivot. Maybe *not* just me.

A sallow teenager sits behind a cash register, tapping at one of those sleek devices Lilou used as a camera. He doesn't look up as I approach. Even after I clear my throat twice, he just keeps tapping like I'm a bothersome ghost who will disappear if he waits long enough.

"Excuse me?" I say finally.

The teenager peers blankly over the register. It takes his gaze a second to focus on me. "What?" he says. "What do you want?"

Pickles, Shrunken Jim whispers.

"Um . . ." I try to think practically. I point at the biggest jar I can see. "That, please. And . . . do you have chocolate?"

The teenager narrows his eyes, then nods. He continues tapping at his device for a few more minutes until I give an exaggerated cough; then he seems to remember I exist and points me toward a shelf of candy. Turns out that four dollars can't buy much, because he takes my coins without giving me change. But that's okay. I walk outside with a humongous jar of pickled eggs that'll last *years* and no fewer than three chocolate bars.

"Thank you!" I call over my shoulder.

The teenager pokes his device and mumbles something that sounds like *stay away*, although it could be *nice day* too.

I chew on a chocolate bar and decide to walk by the watch fires on my way back to the Unnatural History Museum. Maybe a new skeleton bobbed up with the rain. Oliver can't get mad if I *happen* to find myself on the edge of Eelgrass Bog in the middle of chores. I'll say I got lost.

Better than going through town again.

It's easy to find the bog border, even for outsiders. Wick's End is on the smallish side, and there are plenty of signposts pointing to the watch fires—apparently they are a "local heritage attraction." The Unnatural History Museum used to be included on those signposts, except the letters have peeled off and only UN UR STOR EUM remains. So it's just the watch fires for now as I weave past houses, gas stations, and a schoolyard. Hood up. Head down. Just focus on the slap of my rubber boots until the bitter wood-smoke scent and flame crackles tell me I'm getting close.

The nearest houses sit one hundred paces away from the watch fires, on account of the wooden rooftops. There are two fires spaced wide apart, like sentinels guarding another world. Each is maybe three times the size of a regular bonfire. According to legend, they've burned for a thousand years without ever going out. People used to believe they kept Wick's End safe from whatever unnatural nastiness lurked on the bog: wraiths and witches and demons. There's even a noticeboard about it, about how the first record of the watch fires appeared in a land survey from 1793, but it's possible they're older than the oldest building in Wick's End. Nobody's sure who created them. They don't even need wood; they just gobble at the peat mud for fuel. It makes the air reek.

Careful. Shrunken Jim winces as we get closer.

"Too hot?"

He grumbles under his breath. He hates the watch fires. Unfortunately for him, the best bones don't turn up this close to Wick's End. We have to go right to the edge.

I trudge along the footpath. The ground is extra soupy today thanks to the rain. As always, my bones shiver with a strange longing that gets bigger and bigger as we approach Eelgrass Bog. I've never crossed beyond the watch fires, but I'm dying to. It's the opposite of how I feel in places like the grocery shop. Like there's something about Eelgrass Bog that wants me to be here, that wants me to explore.

But rules are rules. Oliver—and my parents—forbids it.

Instead, I just look. Eelgrass Bog resembles a foggy farmer's field gone wild, with scraggly grass clumped into tussocks, oozing dark puddles, and thin birch trees clustered on the horizon. But it only *seems* empty. What might be crawling beyond the hazy smoke? How many bones sleep beneath the ground? Are the creatures from Shrunken Jim's stories still there?

Cold wind brushes my cheek as I step closer. I swear it breathes my name: *Kesssss, Kesssssss . . .*

Kess, says Shrunken Jim sharply. *Focus, please.*

"Right." I catch myself. The wind quiets.

Honestly, Shrunken Jim mutters. I'm not sure if he's scolding me or the wind. *Oh! Check that puddle to your left! Is that a bone?*

I wander off the footpath. "No. It's a broken teacup."

How about over there?

"Hmm. No, those're old socks."

What about by those reeds?

"Lapwing feathers."

I hopscotch along the muddy space between the watch fires, not quite in Wick's End, not quite on Eelgrass Bog, inspecting out-of-place objects that usually turn out to be litter or bird poop. I manage to gather a couple of small bones into my backpack, though I'm 99 percent certain they belong to a goose. Just when I'm about to call it quits, voices float through the smoke.

"Can we leave now? I promise it doesn't get better up close."

"Eurgh, my shoes are soaked! Maggie is right. We should turn back."

"Just a little closer? Please?"

I suck in a surprised breath and almost drop the last few bones.

It's Lilou. Here. Walking up the footpath. I'm filthy and rain frizzed, so I try to back away before she notices me. But my boot squelches too loud, and next thing I know, I'm face-to-face with a group of kids in matching school uniforms. For a second, they all wear identical blank expressions as the teenager in the grocery store, like their attention keeps sliding off me same as water off a duck.

Except Lilou.

She stiffens when our gazes meet. Her hair is still in black braids, and she's clutching her flat device, though this time she's wearing a school uniform too, with a neat collar and skirt.

My stomach turns to sludge.

"Hi, Kess," she says politely.

"Who's that, Lils?" a pinch-faced boy sniffs, eyes narrowing when they finally land on me. "Has she got bones in her hand?"

I feel my cheeks redden. *Lils?*

"They're for my Unnatural History Museum." I shove the bones into my backpack. "We . . . um, we always need . . ."

"The *what*? Oh my god, I didn't know we even had one of those," the boy crows. "Unnatural History Museum? Are you serious?"

"It's that messed-up building on Anning Street," a freckled girl says. "I heard my mom complain about it. She said unnatural stuff is cool for tourists and all, but pretending it's real makes the town look bad."

"I can't believe we have weird bonfires and an unnatural history museum but no decent cafés," a kid mutters, glaring balefully at the watch fires like it's their fault for existing. "This place stinks. Literally."

The pinch-faced boy, however, looks at me with a sharp new interest. "Do you live in the museum? Do you have to share your room with dead bodies?"

"Mummies," I mutter. "Not the same."

"It kind of is, though. Elliott is right," the freckled girl says.

"Is that what you're doing out here? Digging up bodies for your creepy museum?"

A hole inside my heart yawns, cold and dark. Technically I *am* looking for dead things, but even I can understand when a question isn't supposed to be answered. I mumble about going home under my breath and try to push past the group, when the pinch-faced boy—Elliott—grabs my arm.

"You should stay," he says, syrupy sweet. "I bet you're an expert on Eelgrass Bog, right?"

"Mostly," I whisper.

"Like, apparently they used these fires to burn witches, back in the day." Elliott grins widely. "Legend says you can still hear their ghosts screaming."

A shiver strokes down my neck. I've never heard that story before, and it freaks me out more than Shrunken Jim's demon tales, for reasons I can't put my finger on. Maybe just because it's cruel. "They didn't burn witches in Wick's End," I say. "The watch fires are meant to protect people, not hurt them."

Somebody snorts.

Firelight flickers across the angles of Elliott's face. He's still looking at me, and I wish he wasn't. I wish he'd go back to acting like I'm invisible. "Go on, Bone Girl," he tells me. "What do the watch fires protect us from?"

"Unnatural things. Like . . . like . . ." My words stutter. An ember spits onto my sleeve, and I jump.

"Aw. Are you afraid?" Elliott says with fake sympathy. "You don't actually believe in ghosts, do you?"

"Elliott," Lilou says sharply. "Leave her alone."

He shrugs. "It's just a question."

"I'm not afraid." My voice sounds small. Too small. I don't enjoy feeling lonely and overlooked, but this is the wrong kind of attention. It makes me want to fold into myself and disappear.

"Cool." Elliott's lip curls. "But just to make sure, I dare you to cross into Eelgrass Bog. All the way. Then we'll see if any witches come to break your neck or whatever."

I have a better idea, Shrunken Jim says. *Punch him and run.*

But Lilou is watching me. They all are—and properly, this time. It's a challenge, a test, and part of me is already imagining what might happen if I pass. Besides, I get the feeling these kids won't let me walk away easily.

I straighten my shoulders. "Fine."

"Go on, then."

"You don't have to," Lilou says. "Seriously, just—"

"*Go on*," Elliott repeats, louder, crossing his arms.

Before I really understand what I'm doing, I step toward the bog. My blood fizzes like it's full of lightning bugs, and my heart pounds loud, almost as loud as Shrunken Jim hissing, *What on earth, Kess! Turn around! We can't!*

Except I can. There's no wall, no fence, nothing but an invisible line in the dirt drawn between the two watch fires. Most people don't cross simply because there's no footpath. Why wade through ankle-deep muck when there's nothing out there but emptiness?

I curl my fingers into fists. *Courage*, I think. If Mam and Da can travel to the frozen ends of the world, I can step into Eelgrass Bog.

Kester Wynn Pedrock, Shrunken Jim yells. *Turn around this instant, or so help me, I won't tell you another Drowned World story ever again!*

"Relax," I mutter under my shaky breath. "It's only one step."

Don't you understand what the watch fires are for? he snaps. *Cursed things aren't supposed to pass between them! If I—if you—*

"Hurry up!" Elliott says loudly.

I clench my fists tighter, feeling all their eyes boring into my back like knives. My feet move faster. I'll show them. I'm not afraid. The watch fires are stinking and hot on either side of me. One more step should do the trick—

Boom!

The flames flare dark red. Embers explode in all directions. The schoolkids leap back, shrieking. My eyes water from the smoke, and I stumble away from the bog, coughing.

Told you, says Shrunken Jim tiredly.

"I'm on fire!" a boy yelps, swatting at his blazer even though the embers barely touched him. "C'mon, let's get out of here. I *knew* this place was weird!"

The others mutter in agreement and hurry toward the foot-path, casting wary glances over their shoulders at the watch fires like they might flare again. Elliott runs the fastest. Only Lilou lingers behind. She stares at me with a furrowed brow, as though she wants to ask a question.

I stare right back. Not on purpose. I'm just numb from the shock of almost getting incinerated. I've never thought of Shrunken Jim as being the type of cursed creature the watch fires are supposed to protect us from. And I guess I hadn't expected their defenses to still work quite so . . . enthusiastically. If I'd been any closer to the flames, I could've blown myself up.

Ice winds through my veins. Maybe there's more truth to Shrunken Jim's and Oliver's warnings than I always thought.

Maybe Eelgrass Bog really is too dangerous for exploring.

5

I barrel through the Unnatural History Museum's front doors, hard enough that a doorknob breaks loose and clatters to the ground. I throw my backpack down, ignoring Shrunken Jim's protests, and go straight to Oliver's library.

"Ollie!" I try to go inside, but the door is locked, as always. "Oliver, open up right now!"

No answer. I press my ear to the wood. There are creaking footsteps inside, so he's definitely here. My throat squeezes like I'm trapped in a bad dream, waiting for Mam and Da to tell me it's okay. Nothing bad actually happened, except almost getting exploded, of course. But my heart continues to pound, pound, pound as I remember those schoolkids laughing at the museum—and at me.

"Oliver Pedrock, you open this door!"

The footsteps stop. Oliver slips into the hallway, immediately shutting the door behind him. His mouth pinches as he takes in my mud-splattered appearance.

"You've been near Eelgrass Bog again," he says in disgust. "How many times do I need to tell you before you listen?"

"I know, I know, I'm sorry. It's just—"

He crosses his spindly arms. "Just?"

"They're—The fires—They told me—But it's *wrong*—"

Oliver studies me for a long moment. Then, quietly, he says, "Did someone say something to you, Kess?"

Yes. No. Suddenly my words turn sticky, and I can't find my tongue. I can't think of a way to explain how awful it felt to hear those schoolkids sneer at the museum. Or how the watch fires flaring felt like a betrayal from Eelgrass Bog itself. Or how all of this is only *part* of the problem, how everything seems to be breaking down. But because Oliver seems ready to listen to me for once, I take a breath and try to explain anyway.

"Our supply money is almost gone," I say. "I—I can't keep up with how fast the museum is wearing down. If I can't get new bones from Eelgrass . . . if nobody in Wick's End takes us seriously . . . I mean, without visitors, everything Mam and Da built will fall apart."

Guilt flashes across Oliver's face. "It won't come to that," he says unconvincingly. "Mam and Da will deal with everything when they come back."

"But when *are* they coming back?"

He looks away. "Kester, we've spoken about this."

"We haven't. You never tell me anything."

"Because you're a child," he snaps, like there aren't only three years between us. "For starters, you keep listening to that ridiculous pickled head more than me. Whenever I *do* tell you something, it's just questions and questions and more questions. So, listen properly this time: Mam and Da will come back when they're ready. Not before."

"But–" A sharp headache stabs at my temples. "They've been gone for ages."

"No, it only *feels* like ages." His voice seems robotic. "Remember, our parents are doing important research. They were hired to investigate those Antarctic skeletons properly; they can't come home until their company decides their work is finished." Oliver tugs at a loose button on his cuff, and he seems to warm again. "Be patient, okay?"

He turns back to the library. Before he can disappear behind his locked door, I catch his elbow.

"Please," I say. "We don't have to keep waiting to fix everything up. We can do it ourselves! If you help me find new bones, we can bring visitors back in no time. I know we can. It'll be just like before."

We both glance at a nearby photograph on the wall, showing the Unnatural History Museum before our parents left. Polished floors. Gleaming exhibits. Visitors in elegant clothes crowding the halls. Even the colors seemed brighter then, as if the photograph is a window to the real world, and we're the ones stuck inside some faded frame. Nobody sneered at us then.

"Please," I say again.

Oliver sighs. "I–I can't."

"Can't what?"

His expression closes off, and he shoves me away. "Can't keep putting up with your whining. You aren't the only one with things to do around here."

With that, he storms back into the library. The lock clicks into place.

"Fine," I say. My voice cracks, and—annoyingly—my eyes are hot and wet. It's annoying because I don't feel sad. I feel *angry*, a furious, boiling sort of angry that twists my insides into corkscrews. A scream is trying to crawl up my throat. But it must get stuck, because the next time I open my mouth, all that comes out is a sob.

Oliver really isn't going to help.

I pace around the museum over a dozen times, up and down the stairs, waiting for my cobweb-brain to churn out a plan. No use staying angry. Oliver can have his paperwork. It's down to me to bring the museum back to life—before the money and our reputation are gone for good. I'm still filthy with mud, treading footprints over the newly swept floors, but I can't stop. Can't rest. I have to think, think, think.

Skulls and vermin, Kess, Shrunken Jim sighs. *Can you stay still for one minute? You're making me dizzy.*

"No," I say. "What if we . . . um . . ."

Put Oliver's head in a jar and sell it to buy fresh paint?

"Not helpful, Jim."

Hmm. I'm sure it'd make you feel better.

I collapse onto a bench in the Hall of Curses, next to a scratched-up display case full of tusked squid. Liquid from their jars has leaked through the cracks and seeped into a bench, giving the whole area a cloying chemical stench. A couple of flies hover over the puddle. I take a few chemical-y breaths, in and out, in and out, until my prickles shrink into my toes and my heartbeat calms.

"We just have to work smarter," I say determinedly. "There's got to be safer ways to find skeletons around Eelgrass Bog—"

Honestly. Shrunken Jim sounds peeved. *We don't need Eelgrass Bog to find bones.*

I dig my nails into the bench's arms, remembering the boom of the watch fires. The scoffs of the schoolkids. *I didn't know we even had one of those,* they said about the museum. *I heard my mom complain about it.* My confidence shrivels. Will monster bones be enough anymore? What would Mam and Da do, if they were here? I can see them smiling from their photographs on the wall, as though they still believe in a part of me that's wrapped up tight with cobwebs and forgetfulness, as though they still trust me to protect everything they left behind. I'm not sure if their trust makes me feel braver or sadder.

The doorbell rings.

I jump to my feet. "A visitor?"

Hey! Hey, don't forget me!

I scoop up Shrunken Jim and run downstairs as fast as I can. There's nobody on the doorstep when I check, and I wonder if I'm losing my skull stuffing for real. Then I see the box.

It's barely the size of my palm, made from polished redwood. The catch is shaped like a crescent moon. When I pick it up, the lid pops open. Inside, nestled into a blue velvet lining, is a perfect skeleton: a bird with slender wing bones and a pearly skull. A note is folded beside it:

> **Meet me @ the mulberry tree.**
> **Sundown.**
> **I have a secret for you.**

Psh, Shrunken Jim says, wrinkling his face. *Those kids are playing games with you. I've always hated riddles.*

I stroke the velvet. My fingers tremble a little. "I don't think it's a game, Jim."

Perhaps I'm just an old head, but who would drop a bird skeleton on our doorstep? The note isn't signed. Secrets are tricky things, you know.

"But it isn't just any bird," I say. "It's a starling."

Huh?

"Like Lilou." My lips tug upward. "Lilou Starling."

The Mulberry Tree died about a hundred years ago. It stands in the center of Wick's End, crooked and hunched like an old man. Thick swaths of ivy have wrapped around the trunk, so if you didn't know any better, you'd think the Mulberry Tree was alive and well. It's also the second closest thing Wick's End has to a famous landmark, besides the watch fires, because it's been standing since ancient times. Even now, sorry-looking as it is, I can feel whispers of old stories creaking through the branches.

"Kess!" Lilou sets down her device, looking relieved. "I'm so glad you came."

Despite everything, a melted-ice-cream sensation pools into my stomach. Raindrops have caught in her eyelashes, and her cheeks dimple when she smiles. I can hardly believe she wanted to see me, on purpose. Either this is a very mean prank, or small dreams can come true.

I stare at my feet. "Thanks for the box. And the bird."

"They were my grandpa's," Lilou says. "He loved birds. He collected everything bird-related he could find, especially starlings—what with our last name and all. I figured you'd appreciate it better than most."

A blush curls under my skin. "It is beautiful."

"Yeah, well, I shouldn't have let everyone tease you like that today. And I shouldn't have acted so weirdly when I visited your museum."

"It's okay." I shrug. "I'm used to it."

"You shouldn't have to get used to it," Lilou says firmly. "Thing is, I thought I needed Elliott and the others' help. Unfortunately most of them have cheese puffs for brains. Either they don't give two figs about Eelgrass Bog, or they're way more afraid than they'd ever admit."

"Most people are, I reckon."

"You aren't."

I don't say anything, because of course I want Lilou to think I'm brave. But that's not always true. If I'd been *really* brave, I would've tried to cross the watch fires before, without needing some boy to dare me in the first place.

"When I met you, I figured you'd be more superstitious than the rest," Lilou says, matter-of-fact. "But the stuff in your museum was real, and I guess knowing makes you less afraid of things, right?"

"Sure," I lie. "Me and Eelgrass are like old friends."

Lilou smiles, flashing her silvery braces. "Which is exactly why I need you, Kess."

"You . . . need *me*?"

She nods. "See, my family is originally from Wick's End. Grandpa grew up here before moving to Ontario, where I was born. When he got sick, he convinced us to move back; he said it was better for us than living in a big city. But just before he died, he told me he had unfinished business here in Wick's End. Stuff my dads wouldn't understand."

I lean beside Lilou, close as I dare. The Mulberry Tree's bark is slimy and smells like damp earth. "What was the unfinished business?"

Lilou glances over her shoulder. "Can you keep a secret, Kess?"

"Yes," I say immediately.

"I mean it. This secret might have teeth. I need to be sure I can trust you."

She watches me seriously, wet hair plastered like cracks across her forehead, and I already know my answer.

"Yes," I repeat. "I can keep a secret."

Lilou grins wide. "Do you recognize this map?"

She unfurls a rolled-up piece of parchment and gives it to me. It feels old, like it might disintegrate at any second, and the ink has smudged and streaked the map with purple lines.

I adjust my glasses. A little dot is marked *Wick's End* in neat handwriting. There's a river trailing off into the far corners of the map, and an X shape drawn on the western side. A signature in the very bottom reads *Property of Jules E. Starling: Positively DO NOT SHARE.*

"It's Eelgrass Bog," I say.

Lilou claps her hands, delighted. "Exactly! You recognized it!"

"And Jules Starling was your grandpa?"

She makes a *ding-ding* noise, which I think means yes. "This map was his last gift to me," she explains. "He was very sick toward the end, but he left instructions, kinda, on the reverse side. Have a look."

Obediently, I flip the map over. There's a rough sketch of a one-antlered stag's head with two crossed pens underneath and three messily written lines:

> *Beware the witches.*
> *Break the curse.*
> *Save the society.*

"Um. What does it mean?" I ask. "What witches? What curse? What society?"

"Well, I can answer *one* of those questions," Lilou says. "Grandpa was obsessed with that stag symbol. When he got sick, he started drawing it all over the place: on napkins, inside books, even on the bathroom mirror. After we moved to Wick's End, he kept talking about how he needed to return to the bog because there was something important he hadn't done. Something about his *society*." Lilou talks breathlessly, like she's been rehearsing what to say for a very long time. "So I did some googling—"

"Googling?" I say blankly.

Lilou gives me a bewildered stare. "The internet, Kess. Don't you have Wi-Fi in your museum?"

"Oh, right," I say. "Of course. Yes."

"Anyway," she continues more uncertainly, "there was nothing online. But after he died, when we sorted through his things, I found some of his old notebooks—including a message about the symbol. Turns out the one-antlered stag was the mark of the Endling Society."

"The Endling Society?" I echo. The name drips off my tongue like a flavor I've tasted before, somewhere murky and long ago.

"He didn't write down many details. From what I could tell, they operated in Wick's End about seventy years ago. Grandpa would've been in high school, but I bet the members were really young and brilliant."

Shrunken Jim scoffs. I nudge his jar with my elbow. This is a big deal for Lilou; I can tell by the way she's bouncing on her heels and fiddling with the toggles on her coat, like she doesn't want me to know how much this matters to her yet. Mam is the same. Whenever she finds a new specimen, she tries to act as though she isn't excited until she has proven it's authentic. Anyway, Lilou's eagerness is contagious. A strange thrill buzzes over my skin as though my body already knows this is going to be really, really exciting.

I clear my throat. "So your grandpa wanted you to save the Endling Society? From some kind of curse?"

"There's no such thing as *actual* curses." Lilou rolls up the map and tucks it away before the rain soaks through. "But you see, Grandpa didn't just collect bird bones. He had lots of . . ." She pauses, searching for the right word. "*Curiosities.* Rocks that changed shape. Cut flowers that never died. Of course, there must be a rational explanation for it all, something to do with chemistry or genetic makeup. Point is, Grandpa was interested in puzzling out the unnatural, and I bet the Endling Society was too." She digs around in her satchel and hands me a stack of letters bound with fraying twine. "Somebody spilled coffee on these, so they're pretty impossible to read, but . . . well, look."

I fix my glasses. Then I have to bite down a gasp. The pages are mostly ruined, but I can still make out a couple of phrases in Grandpa Starling's handwriting:

> *The Proprietors of the Unnatural History*
> *Museum . . . won't be able to return . . . Eelgrass*
> *Bog . . . so very sorry . . . tell them that nobody . . .*
> *megafauna, perhaps cursed . . . for the Endling*
> *Society to continue.*

I gape at Lilou. "He wrote letters to our museum?"

Her lips quirk. "Technically. He never sent them. But it's another piece of the riddle. Maybe the Endling Society found something dangerous, something they couldn't explain, and they were searching for people who could help. I'm not sure why he kept them, though."

The Proprietors of the Unnatural History Museum. Goose bumps ripple down my arms.

"Perhaps he knew my parents," I say eagerly.

"Maybe." Lilou shrugs. "But these letters were probably before their time. They look pretty old. Who owned the museum before your parents? Your grandparents?"

"Oh. Um. I guess so," I say, even though it's not something I've really thought about before. Whenever I think about the Unnatural History Museum *before* my parents, the memories are fogged and blurry. I can't imagine the building without them.

"Grandpa was very, very secretive," Lilou continues, "but if he wanted me to save the Endling Society—maybe from something they found—then members must still be around. I think the X on the map is a clue to help us track them down. And whatever that clue is, it's hidden on Eelgrass Bog. Which is where you come in, Kess."

A wind plucks at the letters, and I hold them tight to my chest so they don't blow away. "You want me to come with you to Eelgrass Bog?"

No, says Shrunken Jim urgently.

"Yes," Lilou says, eyes gleaming. She reaches out to grab my wrist. "It's easy to find digital maps of Eelgrass Bog, but there aren't any footpaths, and the maps in your museum didn't have any new information. Plus, I don't want to go alone. You've grown up surrounded by stuff from Eelgrass! Who better to help me than someone who's interested in the unnatural, same as Grandpa? Same as the Endling Society?"

I stare at her hand, clasped around mine. She quickly lets go.

"Of course, you don't have to," she adds. "Grandpa was kinda vague, so perhaps I'm wrong, and there's nothing to find at all. But it could be fun?"

Tell her the truth, Shrunken Jim growls. *You've never stepped more than a foot in Eelgrass Bog, and you aren't about to start now. Listen to Grandpa Starling! "Beware the witches!" You could both end up in pickle jars too!*

The rain starts coming down harder. The Mulberry Tree creaks like a haunted house. I wipe off my glasses and say, slowly, "What if the Endling Society actually was involved in something dangerous? Like what the legends warn about, the witches or ghosts or human-eating puddles?"

"Ghost stories aren't about actual ghosts," Lilou says reasonably, as though she's done lots of research on the matter. "Long ago, perhaps someone drowned in the river. Then people started talking about how the mud *ate* them. A witch could be anyone who acts differently. Anyway, Grandpa wouldn't send me on a quest into certain doom."

I glance at the letters again. *To the Proprietors of the Unnatural History Museum.* Grandpa Starling was writing to Mam and Da. If Lilou is right, and the Endling Society was interested in the unnatural, then it makes sense for them to know about my parents. Maybe Mam and Da knew about the Endling Society too. The bubbling thrill inside me grows bigger. If I help Lilou find the Endling Society, if we save them from whatever mess they

52

are involved with, they'd be grateful to us. I could ask them what they know about the unnatural side of Eelgrass Bog. They could steer me toward something wonderful and strange and secret, something big enough to save the Unnatural History Museum once and for all.

"Take some time to decide," Lilou says. "It's a lot to ask, and if you're uncomfortable . . ."

"I'm not afraid," I say.

Kess, Shrunken Jim hisses. *Be reasonable. Vermin's sake, what are adventures worth if you're flesh-stripped bog chow? I won't be able to go with you and—*

Shrunken Jim stops, suddenly, like he's said too much. But he's too late. I already figured it out.

The watch fires flared because they're supposed to stop cursed things from passing back and forth . . . which means they flared because of Shrunken Jim. Not me. If I leave him behind, I should be able to cross over without trouble.

Shrunken Jim splutters like he's read my thoughts. *No, that's not . . . I didn't mean . . . You can't possibly survive without a guide! You'll die!*

I grind my teeth. Truth is, the Unnatural History Museum needs my courage.

Maybe Eelgrass Bog gobbles people.

Maybe not.

Either way, maybe it's time to follow in my parents' footsteps and find out for real.

"All right," I say determinedly. "Let's do it."

6

Lilou's smile is as bright and sharp as a thunderstorm, maybe the realest smile she's given me so far. It's not hard to imagine her grandpa as a genius secret society member. "Meet you at the watch fires tomorrow at twelve o'clock?"

"Tomorrow," I echo.

Her smile widens. "I knew I could count on you, Kess Pedrock." Then she checks the screen of her device and curses. "Sorry, gotta run. Bye!"

I watch her go until she's rounded a corner, then wind my way back to the Unnatural History Museum.

"Well?" I say to Shrunken Jim. He's silent, but there's no way he'll stay quiet about our new plan. "Are you angry?"

You're a silly, foolish girl, he says, voice tight and definitely brimming with anger. *Just because you're desperate to impress Miss Starling—*

"Am not!"

—doesn't mean you can go gallivanting off to Eelgrass Bog. Grandpa Starling was clearly off his rocker. There's an entire room in your museum full of creatures that got stuck in the bog and mummified, for vermin's sake! It isn't a playground!

I roll my eyes. "Not everyone gets turned into mummies, Jim."

Your parents are experienced scientists. You're a kid. You have no idea what you'll find out there.

"Suppose you do?"

Shrunken Jim peers up at me. *Yes. And I've already died once, which is enough for a lifetime, thank you very much.*

"Three hundred years ago."

He scowls. *Haven't I told you about the many, many ways Eelgrass Bog can kill you? Drowning, starvation, exposure, wayward ghosts, cannibal witches, not to mention how dangerous curses can be—*

"Okay, okay," I say. I don't want to argue, not when he sounds so much like Oliver. Anyway, I can make my own decisions.

And I can be brave like Mam and Da.

Once I'm back at the Unnatural History Museum, I prepare a rucksack with my magnification goggles, spare socks, two remaining chocolate bars, and a paper bag for bones. I consider bringing one of Mam's penknives, but knives probably don't work too well against ghouls and witches. Plus, I've never used a knife for anything except buttering toast before.

As night creeps in, I slip into my pajamas. "Will you wake me up when it's time to go, Jim?"

No, he says stubbornly. *You aren't going to Eelgrass Bog.*

"Yes I am."

Aren't.

I sigh. My alarm clock takes a couple of bashes to start ticking again, but I manage to set an alarm for eleven o'clock tomorrow morning.

It takes a long time to fall asleep, because my heart hasn't stopped drumming. When my eyes finally close, I dream of my parents, as always. No, not a dream—a memory. A picnic. We had a blanket spread across the museum's rooftop, our backs against a crooked chimney. Mam was setting out her famous blackberry-and-honey sandwiches. Da was somewhere nearby, singing, *Take my hand, oh my darling; we'll outrun the dark. Don't go away now; you have stolen my heart.*

I sat tucked up close to Oliver.

"See the bog, Kess?" he said, pointing into the mist. "That's where the megafauna once lived. Monstrous snakes. Rats the size of mammoths. Fish that made whales look like minnows. Bloodthirsty witches who made live-forever charms using their hearts."

"You've told me a thousand times," I said. "Da tells it scarier than you."

"How does Da tell it?"

"He said Wick's End was built on an underground lake that's so deep, it goes all the way to the bottom of the world. There's drowned things down there, crawling with maggots, things that'd steal your skin and teeth if they got the chance. It isn't the bog that's carnivorous. It's the stuff that lives underneath."

Oliver chuckled, wrapping his arms around his knees. "Okay, you win." He gave me a side-eye. "You know it's not true, right? There's nothing under Eelgrass Bog except bones."

"Unnatural bones?"

Before he could answer, Mam handed us each a plate of

sandwiches. I was about to cram as many into my mouth as possible when—

My alarm clock shrieks like someone is tearing it apart.

I groan and clamp a pillow over my ears. Sunshine spills over my bedsheets, watery yellow. My heart beats too slowly, as though it hasn't woken up with the rest of me. *Thud-nothing. Thud-nothing. Thud-nothing.* I know it's already late, but if I wasn't so excited to explore with Lilou, I might've gone back to sleep for a couple more hours.

It takes several tries to button my crimson cardigan. Then I realize I've put my pants on backward. I don't even try to wear a ponytail, settling on a quick comb-through instead to get rid of the snarls.

Shrunken Jim glares at me from the windowsill when I open the curtains. *You're still serious about this?*

"Yep." I yawn. "You can't stop me."

I know. Shrunken Jim sounds tired, like he hasn't slept a wink in centuries. Even his mouth-stitches sag. *I've never been able to stop you.*

I pause halfway through pulling on my rubber boots. "What's that supposed to mean?"

Nothing. He sighs. *It's just . . . there's so much you don't understand about Eelgrass Bog. And I won't be there to help keep you safe.*

"I'll be sensible. Promise. You don't have to worry about me."

Shrunken Jim avoids my gaze. *Of course, I wouldn't need to worry if you stayed.*

I set my jaw. "I have to go, Jim. I promised Lilou, and if we find the Endling Society, they'll help us save the Unnatural History Museum. I can feel it."

Always the museum, Shrunken Jim mutters. *A building and the ravings of an old man, eh? That's what you're risking your life for?*

"It's not just a building," I say frostily. "It's home."

It can be replaced. You can't.

But he's wrong. The Unnatural History Museum can't be replaced. I'm annoyed he'd even suggest it. Losing it would break Mam's and Da's hearts.

"Won't be long," I say, like I'm off on grocery chores. Someone has to keep the mood light around here. "If I die, remember to blame Oliver for me."

Kess—

I grab my rucksack and hurry downstairs before he can say anything else to make me change my mind. The exhibits look extra drab today, and I almost feel guilty about leaving instead of cleaning. But cobwebs can be dusted later. An unnatural new discovery will bring back visitors, and that will fix everything.

I don't even pause when I pass Oliver's bedroom. He'd go berserk if I told him where I was going. Besides, he made it perfectly clear how little he cares for our future. I drop the gigantic jar of eggs in front of the library door in case he gets hungry and leave without looking back.

Lilou is waiting by the watch fires, drawing squiggles in the mud with a stick. A camera hangs around her neck—a proper one this time—and her pockets are stuffed with notebooks, pencils, and a tube-shaped flashlight. When she sees me, she tosses the stick. "Hey, Kess! Are you okay? You look tired."

"Oh, I'm fine," I say.

I *am* fine. My heart is back to a regular pace, less hollow than usual. My cheeks tingle red, and it isn't because of the watch fires. Lilou makes me feel *here*, when everyone else makes me feel like I'm about to fade away.

I shake my head. *Focus.*

"What're the squiggles for?"

She winces. "It's yesterday's math homework. We're starting long division, which is actually pretty fun once you get the hang of remainders, and whenever I've got free time, I try to understand—" She bites her tongue. "Sorry. It's really boring."

"No it's not! When I draw squiggles, they're plain nonsense," I say. "This is way better."

Lilou smiles. "It's a puzzle, I guess. That's how Grandpa taught it to me."

"My parents love puzzles too," I say. "I bet they'd have been friends with your grandpa."

"Yeah," Lilou says, a little sadly. "He was easy to like."

We shuffle closer together and peer beyond the watch fires. Flames make shadows dance through the air like long-limbed monsters. A wall of fog chokes out the sun, and I can't see more than a few feet. Just fields of wild grass and puddles.

"I've got a compass on my phone," Lilou says, "so we shouldn't get lost. I did some calculations with Grandpa's map, and that X shouldn't be more than an hour's walk from Wick's End."

"Okay." I raise my leg, and the mud squelches, leaving a soupy footprint behind. "Guess we can always retrace our footsteps if we get lost, right?"

Lilou nods brightly.

I squint at the fog. The boundary line between Eelgrass Bog and Wick's End is barely a dozen steps away, and it feels like we're standing at the lip of a bottomless chasm. It's dizzying, how much I want *and* don't want to cross over. My skin prickles as I remember how the watch fires flared last time I was here. Even if Shrunken Jim isn't going to be with me this time, I don't entirely trust the fires not to explode us both.

Lilou takes the first step. She glances back at me. "Coming, Kess?"

I breathe deep and cough. Gosh, that smoke is thick. But I step up to Lilou, and we go forward together, wading through the fog. Step. Step. Step. We step and keep stepping until the watch fires stand on either side of us. They flare ever so slightly red as we cross, spitting embers, but not nearly as bad as when Shrunken Jim was with me. In fact, once we're on the other side, I wonder if I imagined the flare completely.

The other side. My blood chills.

Somehow, just like that, we're on Eelgrass Bog.

7

Eelgrass Bog is incredible. It doesn't *look* incredible, with nothing except dark mud and scraggly tussocks in all directions, but as soon as we cross over, I feel a lift in my chest I can't explain. There's a peculiar power here. Something old. Something always. I have the strangest sensation of returning to a place I used to belong.

I tip back my head and twirl. "It's so giant!" My voice echoes through the fog until it sounds like the whole world is shouting back at me: *Giant, giant, giant!* It makes me want to howl and dance and run. The wind yanks at my coat, and I whoop as loudly as I can. No one tells me to shut up. No one looks at me funny. The wind just gusts harder until I could almost lift off the ground. I feel like I could fly.

"Want to know exactly how giant this place is?" Lilou asks. "You could fit over a thousand Central Parks in Eelgrass Bog. That's four hundred thousand football fields. Bigger than most cities!"

"Wow," I say, spinning faster and faster until my glasses slip. "How'd anyone figure that out?"

Lilou squats and snaps a photograph of a curious lapwing bird that's wading through the grass. "Math is a puzzle, remember?

That's what Grandpa said. You can take anything in the universe and turn it into numbers, if you know how. Like magic."

I suppose that's true. Numbers don't have teeth or claws or glow-in-the-dark scales; they can't tell stories or give you nightmares. But that doesn't mean they can't be magical. And I guess there is something scary about big numbers, if you consider them hard enough.

I straighten my glasses and tromp beside Lilou. "What now?"

"Well, we haven't been gobbled yet," she says. I can't tell if she's teasing or not. She pulls out her flat device and angles it toward me. "We're about here, see?"

There's another map on the device's screen, so clear it looks like a photograph. It shows Eelgrass Bog from above, same as her grandpa's map, except this version also shows the endless green-and-brown surface, cracked in half by the river. It even shows where the larger puddles and birch thickets are. It *must* be a photo, though I have no idea how anyone managed to hold a camera so high, unless it was somehow taken from an airplane.

"Wow," I breathe.

Lilou chuckles. "Obviously we can't see the X-mark on the phone. But it's a bit easier to tell exactly where we are."

"That's a *phone*?" I'm seriously impressed. Our phone at the Unnatural History Museum doesn't have any kind of screen, let alone one with *maps*. You can't take it anywhere because of its cord.

Lilou gives me a funny side-eye. "Um. Yes? Haven't you seen a phone before?"

"Oh, sure," I say hurriedly. "It's just, ours is . . . bigger."

This must be the right thing to say, because she laughs. "Yeah, I'm really hoping for a better one when I turn thirteen."

I nod and try to imagine how much more a phone could possibly do.

Lilou pops it into her pocket. "Guess we have to go that way."

Of course there are no pathways on Eelgrass Bog, no signposts pointing THIS WAY TO FIND THE ENDLING SOCIETY. But the wind tugs us onward as sure as ships in the sea, and I realize I'm not worried about getting lost at all. Maybe that's the real magic of Eelgrass Bog: it feels like nothing can go wrong, so long as we keep moving onward. That doesn't mean it's easy going. Sometimes the puddles are near invisible and suddenly swallow my legs. Fat blackflies swarm around my head. And no matter where I look, there aren't any bones.

Yet. Something will surface eventually. And if it doesn't, the Endling Society will surely have something for us after we help them.

But we walk and walk and walk, boots *pop-thuck*ing with every step. My heart hums like it's waking from a too-long sleep. We reach a puddle the size of a small lake and have to jump across on mossy stones. I turn back to Lilou, hand outstretched. She could easily jump onto the next stone, but she knots her fingers with mine and lets herself be pulled forward. She grins at me. Mud is splattered across her nose like freckles or stars.

I don't realize we're still holding hands until she jumps forward, dragging me along. The butterflies in my stomach soar. By the time we've crossed the puddle, my cheeks hurt from smiling, and I decide I could stay here forever. Oliver and Shrunken Jim had no idea what they were talking about. This place is everything.

Then something catches the corner of my eye.

Lilou swats at the flies, panting a little. "What is it?"

"Over there"—I point—"there's a dark patch. But it doesn't look like water."

She stretches onto her tiptoes for a better glimpse. "You're right. Huh."

"We should go there," we say at the same time.

I'm itching to gallop ahead, but Lilou's slowing down as the mud gets soggier. I guess she isn't as used to walking through thick mud as me, and she keeps tripping over the tussocks. I start to ask if she wants to hold my arm for balance. But that might be weird somehow, so I swallow the words down.

At least there's plenty else to focus on. I turn my eyes downward. Worms and feathers and rocks, even some crinkly silver litter that must've blown over from town. But nothing unnatural. If there are bones, they're deep where I'd have to dig to find them—

"Whoa!"

Lilou hauls me backward by my collar. "Jeez, Kess! Careful!"

"Oops," I whisper. Because two more steps and I'd have tumbled into the dark patch, which definitely isn't a puddle. Not even close.

It's a *hole*. A hole that's big enough to devour the Unnatural History Museum with room for leftovers.

Carefully, I peer over the edge. Cold air blows back into my face like the hole is a mouth with *very* sour breath. Peat mud stinks of rotten eggs, and this area stinks worse than usual. I can't see a bottom. Good thing Lilou caught me in time, else I'd still be falling. My stomach somersaults.

"It's a perfect circle," Lilou says, walking slowly around the edge of the hole. "*Too* perfect. Which means it might be man-made, which means..." She yanks out her grandpa's map. "Yes, yes, yes! This is about where the X is! Brilliant! Do you think it's safe to get closer?"

"Um," I say grandly. That rotten peat smell must have tickled its way into my brain and brought the cobwebs back, because I can't think much at all. Just look at how deep and dark the hole is. I'm glad we found the right spot, but my bones have also gone twitchy, like if I'm not careful, they'll jump over the edge without me. Like the hole is sucking me inward.

Lilou drops a pebble in. A few seconds later, there's a wet *thwap*. This makes her frown even more. She grabs her flashlight from her backpack and clicks it on, beaming white light into the darkness. "Oh! It's a tunnel!" she cries. "Look—it slopes away from us!"

Tunnels are good. Tunnels are meant to be climbed in *and* out of. Even if this one has a very, very odd feeling about it. It's spooky. "What d'you think is down there?" I ask.

"No idea," Lilou says, mouth twisted with the same combination of excitement and unease I'm feeling. "But this must be where Grandpa wanted me to go."

"So you want to explore inside?"

"Well," Lilou says, "it probably isn't safe."

"We could come back later with assistance," I suggest, though I have no idea what kind of assistance we'd get.

"Hmm," Lilou hums. "Can't imagine my family trekking out here."

"My brother wouldn't either," I say.

We both edge a little closer. I know what Shrunken Jim would say: *Don't you dare, Kess Pedrock. You are not crawling into a strange tunnel in the middle of Eelgrass Bog! It's a trick. A wolf pit for wayward girls.*

I swallow the lump of unease. "Might be hard to find it again."

"Yes," says Lilou slowly. "And nobody will help unless we tell them about the Endling Society."

Now or never, then. I curl my fists and try to think brave thoughts. It's a tunnel, not an endless hole. It could hold fossils and bones and who knows what else. It could lead us to the people who could save our museum. Mam and Da wouldn't be afraid if they were here. *Courage, Kess.*

I jump.

My knees smack into soft dirt.

A second later, Lilou follows, balancing the flashlight on her shoulder. The air is colder here. Sharper. A rumbling hum comes from deeper down, like all the worms are whispering in a forgotten language. There might be unnatural stuff living underground, demons or goblins or mummified members of the Endling Society. I cup my hands around my mouth and call, "*Hello?*"

Hello! my echo replies. *Hello! Hello! Hello!* No beady eyes blink through the gloom. No monsters uncurl from the shadows.

"Okay," Lilou says, back to business. With her around, at least, nothing feels too badly out of control. "Let's hope we don't get eaten."

We follow the milky flashlight beam farther underground. It's like walking through a cave, except the walls are made of peat instead of rock, and roots curl from the ceiling instead of stalactites. I keep my eyes peeled for bones. Down, down, down we go, until there's no daylight. The deep-earth hum gets louder. My breathing is heavy, like I'm still afraid, which I'm not. I'm *not.* I wonder if there's less oxygen underground.

"We're getting pretty deep," I point out.

"I don't understand what made this," Lilou says. Her breath is coming quicker too. "It doesn't look natural, but it doesn't look dug out either."

"Witches?"

She doesn't answer, probably because she's too polite to tell me that in her opinion, witches aren't real. Even if her grandpa seemed to believe otherwise.

Water drips from the ceiling. Roots stretch longer, trailing across our heads. I imagine we're walking down a gigantic throat into the bog's stomach. My whole body tingles. Despite the depth and the stench and the lightness in my head, I find myself walking faster and faster.

"It goes forever," I puff. "Hope it doesn't dead-end."

Lilou keeps quiet. I glance at her, worried I've accidentally said something wrong again. But she doesn't look angry. Just pale and maybe a little sick.

"Are you okay?" I ask.

"Fine," she says hastily.

"You sure?"

"Just . . . the smell . . ." She swallows. "Shouldn't have had eggs for breakfast."

I reach for her hand but chicken out at the last minute. Anyway, she seems to be concentrating a lot on not throwing up. And I should concentrate more on the tunnel, in case there are bones or signs of the Endling Society. *Something* is down here. Every alarm bell in my usually cobwebby brain is singing, *Onward, onward, onward.*

Then a shimmer catches my eye.

"Can you shine your flashlight over there?" I ask, pointing into the dark.

Lilou nods weakly. The flashlight beam swings around, and she sucks in a startled breath. "What is that?"

Now it's my turn not to answer. Because the shimmer isn't from a bone, or a fossil, or any kind of treasure. It's a *scale.* A gleaming scale the size of a dinner plate. And that's not the wildest part.

The scales are *everywhere.*

This one has been knocked loose, but as Lilou slowly moves her flashlight, more and more become visible behind a thick coat of grime. Above us. On the ground. Hundreds of gigantic scales, coating the tunnel like wallpaper.

"Unreal," Lilou whispers. "What—what do you suppose . . . ?"

My dream from last night creeps to the front of my memory. *See the bog, Kess? That's where the megafauna live.*

"Some people believe there were giant animals living on Eelgrass Bog," I say slowly. "World-serpents with bodies so thick a dozen grown-ups couldn't wrap their arms around them. They lived underground and feasted on magma. Whenever they came too close to the surface, there'd be earthquakes all across the country."

Lilou's skin is ghostly pale. "Who told you that?"

"Oliver," I admit. "And my dad."

"But it's only a story," Lilou says. For the first time, she actually sounds afraid. "Real snakes aren't big enough to make underground tunnels. Earthquakes are caused by tectonic plates. You can't eat magma."

"Well, the snake that made this would be long gone," I say. "This tunnel is at least seventy years old, if your grandpa marked it on a map."

"It *can't* be made by a snake," Lilou says shrilly.

But it can. I've held the bones, heard the tales. Even if this world-serpent died thousands of years before Wick's End laid its first brick, it was still *here*. I stretch my arms wide, feeling how massive the tunnel is, and the tingling spreads right down to my toes.

"Kess," Lilou says.

I've walked away from her without realizing it. When I turn around, Lilou is bent in half. Her breath comes quick and shallow, and the flashlight beam has gone wobbly in her hands.

"Can we get out of here?" she says weakly. "The smell . . . I'm gonna puke."

"What about the Endling Society?"

"Please, Kess. There's something bad down here," she says, and she sounds so scared, I forget about the world-serpent.

Almost. I yank a loose scale from the mud and tuck it in my backpack. Then I loop my arm through Lilou's, and both of us stumble toward the surface.

8

Returning aboveground is like waking from a dream. The sky is a cloudy purple-gray, but after the tunnel, even the dim sunlight is painful. I rub my eyes and take a lungful of fresh air, then another and another until everything feels real again.

Lilou immediately retches into a puddle. "Oh man," she gasps. "*Not* fun."

I wonder if I should hold her hair back. I settle on asking, "Are you okay?"

"Peachy," she mumbles, wiping her mouth on the back of her hand. "Urgh. At least I didn't faint. You would've had to carry me out."

I laugh awkwardly. "Well, the stink *was* pretty bad."

"Maybe that's what's hidden down there. A million rotten eggs." Lilou shudders. "Grandpa has a mean sense of humor."

She's joking, of course. But I can't help picturing a chamber of giant world-serpent eggs hidden away underground, slowly hatching over hundreds of years. Forget skeletons. Imagine having one of *those* in the Unnatural History Museum.

I glance back at the tunnel. Fog has pooled over the ground in a thick gray blanket, and the tunnel is almost invisible. I run my fingertips over the scale in my backpack. "Lilou? Do you really think—"

"Someone's watching us," she interrupts.

I whirl around to follow her gaze. Sure enough there's a person-shaped shadow standing in the fog, barely a stone's throw away. After the tunnel, I'm not feeling afraid of some human, so I step forward to get a better look. It's a man—ruddy cheeked and hawk nosed, with a grizzly beard chewing up most of his face. He wears a patchwork of different leathers clipped together with fishhooks, mussel shells, bone shanks, and pearly drops that can only be fancy earrings. As soon as he catches us looking, he lowers his head and pretends to notice something fascinating on the ground.

He's not quite old enough to be an Endling Society member from seventy years ago, but maybe new members have joined since then. "Excuse me," I say, "are you from Wick's End? You haven't heard of the Endling Society, have you?"

The man spits. Maybe it's my fogged glasses, but it almost looks like it's a worm he spits up. "Dunno what you're gabbling about. You shouldn't've gone down that tunnel, kiddie. Nothing good will come of it."

"Do you . . ." Lilou winces and draws herself upright, shuffling to my side. She still looks kind of green. "Do you know what's down there? My grandpa gave me a map, and he marked this tunnel like it was important."

Lilou tries to remove the map from her rucksack, but the man waves his hands, panicked, as if she's trying to draw a gun.

"No! No, none of that. I promised I wouldn't go back," he cries. "I want nothing t'do with it!"

"With what?"

"I'm a scientist," he says, as though Lilou hadn't spoken. "Been studying Eelgrass Bog for . . ." He counts on his fingers, looking confused. "Well, it doesn't matter. Many years. Peat bogs keep things preserved, you see. It's the humic acid. And the magic, of course, 'cept nobody writes papers on *that* at the university. It's for the best. Some things aren't worth meddling with."

"My parents are also scientists," I tell him. "They studied unnatural things on Eelgrass Bog. Did you know them? Dr. and Dr. Pedrock."

"Never heard of 'em. And tell 'em to stay away." The man spits, and this time I'm even *more* certain there's a worm involved. My stomach twists. "It's a lost cause. I'll be headed home soon, mark my words. Just need a few more samples . . ."

He opens his coat to show an array of cracked glass tubes. Most of them seem to be full of murky bog water, although he's trapped a swarm of live mosquitoes too. My unease grows, and my heart starts to double-tap. There's a shine in the scientist's eye that feels wrong somehow, like he's got threads of the tunnel's shadows hidden beneath his patchwork coat. Like there's something moving inside him that isn't exactly . . . *him.*

Lilou is doing her best to keep a polite smile. "So, um, did you ever study the tunnel? We saw the scales—"

"*No!*" he shouts, and we both jump backward. "It's a witch nest! It's a nightmare hive! That's why I don't meddle with underground nonsense anymore." He angrily jams a finger into his ear and wiggles it. "They burrow into your dreams worse than termites. Every time I sleep, I see them. Horrid things, awful things, nasty things!"

Lilou's smile wavers. "What things?"

"Demons," the man snarls. "Go down there, and they'll crawl into your heads too, mark my words. If you knew what's good for you, you'd run. There's already a witch on your tail."

My heart drops into my toes. I look over my shoulder, but there's nothing except scrubby heather and the nearby maw of the tunnel. It makes me wonder if witches can turn invisible. Then I remember Elliott's words back at the watch fires, about witch burnings and screaming ghosts, and cold spills down my spine. Grandpa Starling's note winks up at me from the top of the rolled-up map: *Beware the witches.*

"Demons don't exist." Lilou's jaw is set. "Grandpa wasn't talking about *real* witches."

"Doesn't matter what you believe," the man says. "They'll creep into your dreams and eat your heart either way." Then he pales like he's scared himself and starts to shuffle off, a grizzled lump of leather and baubles.

As much as I'd like to see the last of him, I'm not ready to give up on answers yet. I ball my fists and cry, "Wait! Can you at least tell us what you know about the tunnel? Was it really made by a world-serpent? When you say 'witch nest,' do you mean—"

The man turns and glares with such venom, I flinch backward a couple of steps. "Questions are knives on Eelgrass Bog," he growls. His breath smells of peat and old mushrooms. "So I will thank you, kiddie, to *stop throwing them at me*. Get back to your little town, you hear? No good comes from sticking your nose into the Drowned World."

He throws his hands in the air with an angry *pah!* for good measure, and before I can open my mouth again, he's vanished into the fog.

Lilou blinks. "What a weird dude."

"Did he say *Drowned World*?"

"He said a lot of garbage. I mean, Grandpa couldn't have been talking about real witches any more than he was talking about a real curse. I figured it was an insult for some of the Endling Society members he fell out with." She looks troubled. "If someone followed us, we would know. Right?"

But my head is too busy spinning to answer. Even with a terrible memory, I've heard enough about the Drowned World from Shrunken Jim to remember what it's supposed to be like. The realm of monsters, megafauna, and golden rivers . . . and the source of everything unnatural on Eelgrass Bog. It seems like the right place for cursed creatures to live. Or for a secret society to hide a dangerous secret.

Goose bumps ripple down my arms. I've always hoped the Drowned World was real. I just never figured I'd find a tunnel that might lead there.

"Kess?" Lilou says.

"No idea," I say quickly. "But actually . . . I think I remembered something in the Unnatural History Museum that might help us."

She brightens. "What is it?"

I think about how baffled she was when I first introduced her to Shrunken Jim and decide she probably doesn't want more unnaturalness at the moment. Not yet. Lilou might not completely believe in fantastical bog stories about witches and monsters, but I've got a feeling we've fallen into one just the same.

"It'll be easier to show you later," I say. "After I've . . . um, checked something."

"Okay." Lilou casts her head skyward and blows out through her teeth. "I suppose we should turn back now anyway. I promised my dads I wouldn't be home too late. They think I'm studying geometry at Madeline's, so . . ."

"So," I agree. I'm both relieved and disappointed to be leaving. The scale sits heavy in my rucksack, and I'm itching to explore the tunnel further, but the scientist's strange warning is stuck in my head: *There's already a witch on your tail.* I still can't see anyone—or anything—through the fog, but that doesn't mean nobody's there.

We're quiet as we walk back toward the watch fires. Lilou's jaw stays tight, and I can practically hear her brain whirring. I focus on the *pop-thuck* of my boots instead of the muddle of unease and excitement quivering through my bones. Stars peer at us from the lavender sky. Bats fly hither-thither like tiny dark comets. Toads croak mournfully. A soda can rolls into a puddle with a *sploosh.* And I don't notice how far we've walked until the scent of the watch fires reaches my nostrils.

Lilou picks up her pace so she's almost running. "Geez, it's good to be back in town!"

A shiver sparks across my skin as I cross into Wick's End. The watch fires flare crimson again, just for a heartbeat, and I swipe an ember from my elbow. Perhaps there's some leftover unnaturalness clinging to us from the tunnel—or that scientist. Lilou seems to be too excited about reaching Wick's End again to notice. I'm also glad to be home safe, though I secretly wish I were still exploring that tunnel. Something important was down there. I know it.

"Guess the mud doesn't eat people after all," I say to distract myself. "You can tell Elliott he was wrong."

"With pleasure." She winces. "Did you hear my stomach just then? I could murder a grilled cheese sandwich."

"Or honey and blackberry."

"Literally anything, to be honest." She wipes a smear of mud from her coat. "Do you want to clean up at my house?"

I blink. "What?"

"You don't have to," she says hastily. "It's just, Dad's grilled cheeses are *really* good, but if you'd rather go straight to your museum—"

"No!" I blurt. "No, that sounds amazing."

Lilou grins, showing off the metal on her teeth. "Great. I'll text my dads and let them know you're coming over."

She taps at her phone as we walk. Mud turns to pavement beneath our feet, and buildings sprout up like weeds. I wonder if the tunnels stretch into Wick's End, if maybe there are serpent scales buried beneath the schoolyard and grocery store. Did Mam and Da know about the tunnels? I curse myself for not asking more questions when I had the chance. Some things feel too big for letters.

But that's a worry for another day. I follow Lilou through the town streets until she turns into a front walk.

We've arrived at Lilou's house.

9

The Starlings' house fits between a terrace of other houses, each as neat and square as the last. If I lived here, I'd need to hang a sign on the door to make sure I didn't forget which redbrick building was supposed to be mine.

Lilou tugs me inside, and I have to blink because everything is so bright. There are more electric lights than I can count. The air smells of flowers and soap and something artificial, and there's cheerful music playing a thousand times clearer than any of my records at home. When I take off my boots, the carpet is fluffy between my toes. No creaky floorboards here.

A man with curly black hair and a knitted sweater offers to hang up my coat before I've finished unbuttoning the toggles. "Nice to meet you, Kess," he says warmly. "I'm Lilou's father, but you can call me Andres."

"Hello," I say. My voice comes out small and shy.

Andres tucks my coat into a neat closet. The doors swish open and closed. "Are you also in Mr. Wienkov's class? I haven't heard Lils mention your name before."

"Kess is homeschooled," Lilou says. "She's really smart."

I flush. "Oh, I'm not–"

"Is Dad around?" Lilou gives Andres a peck on the cheek. "Can he make us grilled cheese?"

"Is that all I'm good for?" another man shouts from across the house. "What happened to *I love you, Dad*, or *Your hair is amazing today, Dad*, or *Let me make* you *a sandwich this time, Dad*?"

"He thinks he's hilarious," Lilou says, rolling her eyes. "Grandpa was the same."

"Almost like they were related," Andres says.

"As you can see"—Lilou looks at me—"I live with clowns. Welcome to the circus."

She leads me into the kitchen and clambers onto a wooden stool, gesturing for me to sit beside her. The countertop is polished like a mirror. It's so *clean*. My reflection stares back at me, wide-eyed, grubby, and dazed. I'm almost too busy gawking to notice the three other people sitting around a table: a gray-haired man and two young kids reading open books.

"Vivienne, Simon, and David, my other dad." Lilou points at each in turn. "Family, meet Kess."

"Why are you dirty?" the smallest kid—Vivienne—says.

"Because we were chased by a witch," Lilou replies without missing a beat. "So we're *really* hungry."

I wait to see if anyone is going to force her to explain. But David just grumbles, "All right, all right. Hint taken. Get the plates out and I'll heat up the pans."

Sometimes, I guess the truth sounds too much like a story to be believed. Anyway, if Lilou's dads are anything like her, they probably don't believe in witches either.

The family jumps into action, chatting and bickering and sizzling thick slices of bread and cheese in a frying pan. It's so . . . *strange*. I can't believe we were trekking across Eelgrass Bog only a short while ago. I feel as though I've tripped into a whole other world, and somehow, this one is more unfamiliar than anything on Eelgrass. It's been ages since I've had a family meal. A pit of loneliness blooms inside my heart.

But soon, I'm distracted by food and decide I can never go back to cockle sandwiches again. The bread I'm given is soft and crispy, and the stringy cheese burns my tongue in the best possible way. I eat so fast, Andres laughs and says, "Wow! Are your parents feeding you at home, Kess?"

He's joking, but my cheeks flush deeper just the same. Lilou nudges my feet reassuringly under the table and warns, "*Dad*, seriously?"

"It's okay." I make myself smile. "My parents are working in Antarctica, so I—I do most of the cooking."

"Antarctica?" David quirks an eyebrow, sliding another sandwich onto my plate. "That must be tough."

"They're strong," I say.

"I meant for you, kiddo. Lilou acts independent, but she'd be lost without her dads at her beck and call." He grins and ruffles her hair. She mouths *sorry* at me, looking mortified. "Who are you living with, then?" he continues. "You got other folks in Wick's End?"

A screen blinks on the refrigerator door. It has a clock with electric numbers instead of hands and a too-bright picture of ice cubes. It reminds me of Lilou's phone. I peel the crusts off my bread, hoping the Starlings don't notice how much I don't belong in their house, and say, "I . . . um, have a brother."

Andres and David share a glance.

"He must be quite a bit older than you," David says carefully.

"Oh, yes. He's great," I lie. "We have a lot of fun together. He . . . he . . . cares."

David's smile is polite. "As long as you're being taken care of."

I nod so forcefully my glasses almost slip off. "He makes me grilled cheese all the time."

Lilou gives me a funny look—but luckily she doesn't call me out. I'm not sure why I'm lying, not when she already knows the truth. Maybe it's something about being here, in this perfect house with this perfect family, that makes me ache more keenly than ever for when *my* family was perfect too. It's like looking into a crystal ball and seeing a vision of everything I've lost. But I don't want the Starlings to believe I'm sad or forgotten. Lying is much easier.

"We're going upstairs now," Lilou announces, licking the last crumbs from her fingertips and sliding away from the countertop. "Thanks for the food, Dad. It was stupendous."

"Give Kess some clean clothes to borrow," Andres says. "You both reek of rotten eggs, for reasons I probably don't want to know."

"Geometry homework," Lilou says, like that explains everything. She gives me a not-so-secretive wink, but even though her dads definitely notice, it doesn't matter. They'd never guess what we've really been up to. Sure enough, Andres just shakes his head and finishes drawing a ketchup smiley face on Simon's plate.

I follow Lilou to her room, which is tucked up behind the kitchen. We go through a door marked LILOULAND, and I'm hit with the scent of sugar cookies. I'm not sure what I expected Lilou's room to look like, and truthfully, I'm a little embarrassed to be here, because this is her private space. But it's... well, lovely. Plastic glow-in-the-dark stars cover the ceiling. Stuffed animals crouch between bookshelves. There's a chalkboard full of swirling math symbols and a lampshade with stenciled ballerinas that leap and flitter like dreams. It's a million miles away from my bone-filled attic.

Lilou catches me looking and winces. "Excuse the mess. It's a bit babyish, but... um..."

"Are you kidding? It's perfect," I say sincerely.

She grins. Her cheeks are the same pink as the walls. "I mean, I don't hate it. Our apartment in Ontario was basically a shoebox. This is way better than sharing with Viv again."

"I'd die if I had to share with Oliver."

"*He's great,*" she mimics. "*We have a lot of fun together.*"

I scowl. "What was I supposed to say?"

"*He's a lazy turnip weevil.* That's what you told me, right?"

"But you're different."

The words slip out heavier than I meant, and an awkward silence drapes across the room. My throat suddenly feels very dry. I pretend to be interested in the ballerina lampshade. It's been a long time since I've had a real human friend. I'm not sure how to *be* a friend. It's like blinking—as soon as I think about it, it becomes harder to act natural.

Lilou kicks at a pillow. "Um, do you want to see more of Grandpa's Endling Society stuff? Now that we know about the tunnels, maybe you'll notice clues I've missed."

I don't think I'll spot anything more than Lilou, but I'm glad for the distraction. She pats the space beside her on the bed. I sit down, cautiously leaving a person-sized gap between us. She mustn't notice, because she just shuffles closer until our knees bump. My whole mouth turns to sand.

"Here." Lilou overturns the contents of an old wooden box onto her lap: papers, photographs, letters. "This is all from his office. My dads gave it to me to sort through. Most of it is ordinary, but there are some interesting diary entries that *might* be referring to the Endling Society."

The paper she gives me is crinkled and patchy—not one paper at all, but several fragments pasted together like a scrapbook page. I squint at the handwriting:

January 25, 1955. *Another wasteful day. P got into a fight with H again. It was funny at first, until H decided she'd had enough and almost sent us home for good. Sometimes it's easy to forget how powerless we are here. P certainly forgets. Then it rained and my tent started to leak, and I cannot find my binoculars. I am very close to abandoning Eelgrass Bog until summertime. Perhaps I shall start a fight with H after all.*

"Who were P and H?" I ask.

Lilou shrugs. "Other members of the Endling Society, I bet. Have you finished reading?"

"Nope," I say. "Almost."

> **March 16, 1955.** *Success! Just kidding. It rained again and someone is stealing my left socks. I suspect you-know-who.*

> **February 7, 1955.** *We dived the river yesterday, hoping to find useful material on a sunken ship. It was called the* Florentina *and there was nothing left aboard except a grumpy conger eel and three sheep skulls. I did not enjoy the dive. Under the silt, the ship rather resembled a sleeping giant and I dreamed that it had woken up and wanted to devour me. P seems to be having nightmares too. H, of course, does not dream.*

> **December 24, 1954.** *Christmas Eve and Eelgrass Bog could not care less. But sunrise was glorious. The world is ours. Sausage for breakfast!*

I flip the paper over, but there's nothing else written down. The sand in my throat has grown into pebbles, and my heart quick-beats as though we're still in the tunnel. Maybe I'm getting a fever.

"Not very useful, is it?" Lilou sighs. "The dates aren't even in the proper order."

Pain needles my temples. The longer I stare at the loopy handwriting, the stranger I feel. There's something *missing*, and although it's impossible, I can't help thinking I should know. If I could only reach through the cobwebs, if I could only think clearly—

"Want to see a photograph of him?" Lilou asks, snapping me back to earth. "Grandpa, I mean?"

"Sure," I say gratefully. I drop the paper into the box as though it's made of dynamite.

Lilou fishes out a stack of photographs, crumpled by a too-tight elastic band. The one she gives me is especially worn. I'm surprised when it shows a teenager instead of an old man. He's got dark, slicked-back hair and delicate features that are almost too pretty to be real, all outfitted up in a school blazer. It's signed *Jules Everett Starling, Wick's End, 1954.* Someone has drawn the Endling Society symbol on the reverse side.

"Obviously he doesn't look like me," Lilou says. "We were all adopted. He's only sixteen here. Can you believe it?"

"Almost Oliver's age," I whisper, a sense of wrongness climbing higher and higher until I can barely breathe. It spills oily down my throat and wraps around my heart, squeezing tight. I should *know*. I should *remember*.

"Suppose so! He hated being photographed. We've got barely any recent pictures, which is a shame because . . ." She trails off and frowns at me. "Kess, are you okay? You've gone really pale."

My hands tremble. Although the picture was taken seventy years ago, and Jules Starling is dead, he seems to be grinning right at me as though I'm seeing him through a window. I jerk to my feet. The picture falls to the floor with a couple of pillows.

"I need to go home," I choke out. "Sorry."

"What? Why?" Lilou says in confusion. She gets up too, reaching for me, but somehow that only makes the twisting inside me worse, and I flinch backward. Hurt sparks in her eyes. "Kess?"

"It's just . . ." I try to explain, but I can't. The cobwebs are too thick. All I can think about is how badly I need fresh air before my whole body goes up in smoke.

She nods uncertainly. "Do you at least want those clean clothes?"

"Sorry," I say again. "Headache."

"Okay." She tries to smile, but I can tell I've hurt her feelings. "Shall I meet you tomorrow morning?"

I nod—at least, I *hope* I nod—then my legs start moving without me. Out of Lilou's room, past where her family is watching television, and as far away from that photograph as I can possibly run.

10

I trip over a broken shingle as I run up the path to the Unnatural History Museum. It must've blown off the roof earlier today. Sure enough, when I pause to glance upward, the roof is peppered with holes where other shingles have gone missing. A pigeon is already trying to build a nest in the exposed rafters below the chimney. We'll be in trouble when it rains.

I kick the shingle into the overgrown hedge. I have no idea how to repair a rooftop, so I don't want to worry about it yet. Not when my head is still spinning like a cyclone.

I stumble through the front doors and trip right into Oliver. For a moment I'm frozen by surprise because he's not in his library. Has he been waiting for me? Has he been worried? Has he seen the pigeons in the rafters and decided to help patch up the museum? I imagine him yanking me into a hug: *I'm sorry I've been so miserable*, he'll say. *Please don't run off again.*

It's okay, I'll reply. *Well, not really. I just saw a photograph that felt like a nightmare, and I don't know why. We found an impossible tunnel on Eelgrass Bog. A witch might've noticed us. Lilou probably thinks I hate her, and somehow that's worse than everything else combined.*

Sounds like you need hot chocolate, Oliver will say. He'll loop his arm through mine, and we'll go to the kitchen; then we'll take our mugs to the rooftop and tell stories until the world makes sense again.

But it doesn't happen like that.

Because Oliver isn't even awake.

He's fallen asleep in an old chair, dust silvering his greasy hair. A line of drool traces down his chin. I don't know what he's doing out here, but it's definitely not worrying about me.

Disappointment curdles with my annoyance. I grab his bony shoulders and shake him, none too gently. "Oliver? Oliver, wake up."

As usual he doesn't listen. His skin is cold and clammy to the touch. If it wasn't for the sluggish *thud-THUMP* of his pulse, I might've thought he was proper dead. Then I really would be alone. But I shake my head, because that's a selfish reason to be relieved that someone isn't dead. I bet Lilou would've already telephoned an ambulance if it was *her* brother unconscious in a chair.

"Oliver," I say, louder. "I went to Eelgrass Bog today."

Nothing.

I smack him across the face. He jerks and lets out a loud snore that echoes around the museum like a thundercrack. But he doesn't wake up. Concern sparks inside me. Oliver is always tired, but this is a very deep slumber, even for him. Is it normal? *Should* I be telephoning an ambulance?

I exhale through my teeth. I'm pretty sure an extra-tired

swamp-vermin brother isn't an emergency. He probably just exhausted himself doing "paperwork." I tuck my concern away and throw his arm around my shoulder. Luckily, he weighs less than an eggshell, and it's easy to lift him up.

I drag him all the way to his library, though I already know the door will be locked. But I rattle the knob just in case and curse when it stays bolted.

It's not fair. My head hurts and my throat is full of pebbles, but instead of taking care of myself, I have to deal with Oliver first.

"Oh, sure," I grunt, dragging him back down the corridor. "We have *lots* of fun together."

His bedroom is up three flights of stairs, so I plop him on a moth-bitten velveteen bench in the Long Gallery instead. Our staircases are too rotten to be carrying anything up there, especially brothers. I check his pulse again. Still not dead. Because it's chilly with all the drafts and broken windows, I figure I'll be nicer than he deserves and fetch a blanket. He's already so cold. I don't want him to become an icicle overnight.

I haul my aching legs upstairs, past exhibits that are sagging and rotting and crumbling. Mummies, fossils, skeletons suspended from rusty wires. Compared to the brightness of Lilou's house, everything seems extra dead, and I can almost, almost understand why people decided our Unnatural History Museum was bad news. Even Eelgrass Bog felt a thousand times more alive than this. If I squeeze my eyes shut, I can trick myself into hearing echoes of Mam and Da laughing with each other, same as David and Andres Starling, but it's garbled and far away like I'm stuck underwater. I open my eyes, and the voices vanish. There's nothing but the creak of rotten wood and Oliver's distant snores.

Shrunken Jim lets loose a shriek as I stagger into my bedroom. *Kess! Brains above, you're alive! What took you so long?*

I smile weakly. "Told you Eelgrass Bog wasn't dangerous."

Are you kidding? You look terrible! Tell me everything!

"Just a minute. I need to grab a blanket for . . ." My smile vanishes. Fragments of bone and wood are scattered across my floor. It's the box Lilou gave me with her grandpa's starling skeleton. Wing bones trail under my desk. The tiny skull has cracked like a nut, as if someone has stepped on it very hard.

My stomach twists sharply. "What . . . what happened?"

Oliver the Opprobrious. Shrunken Jim's mouth-stitches pinch together. *He came up here looking for you. I told him you'd gone to the grocery store, but then he saw that box . . . Well, as you can see, he didn't seem to like it.*

I crouch and gather up the shattered pieces. The stag emblem has been ruined beyond recognition. "Did he say why?" I ask quietly.

Shrunken Jim hesitates. *No. Just that you are, apparently, a "disobedient little toe rag," and he was going to wait by the front door so you couldn't sneak past him when you came home.*

The fist around my stomach clenches tighter. So that was why Oliver was waiting. Not because he was worried. Because he wanted to challenge me about the box, for some reason. I hold the broken bones close to my chest and remind myself to breathe, slow and calm. "Well," I say eventually, "he can forget having a blanket tonight."

He might freeze. Shrunken Jim sounds hopeful.

I set the starling's fragments on my shelf, beside the new world-serpent scale and the rest of my natural bone collection: badgers, hawks, mice. Mam and Da beam down at me from a portrait nestled between two squirrel skeletons. I press my fingers against their smiling faces, swallowing the pebbles down. Oh, I miss them. They always know what to do.

Did something happen? Shrunken Jim asks. *You seem more pensive than usual.*

I sigh. "What does that mean?"

Shrunken Jim bobs his head in a shrug. *Y'know. Thoughtful. Distant. Not quite here. Was Eelgrass Bog disappointing?*

"Not at all," I say. "Actually, it was incredible. I felt good there."

Good?

"Like . . . I belonged, somehow. It's tricky to explain."

Try.

I pull a face. "We don't all have big fancy words like you."

Then use smaller ones. Shrunken Jim sounds grim and serious, as though he's preparing to take notes on everything I say.

"Okay, okay," I say, "just let me get cleaned up first."

I only spend a few minutes in the shower because the water reeks of fishbones and sputters like a choking cat—plus there's a nest of roaches under the sink. Once the dirt is scrubbed away, I change into a fresh pair of Mam's patchwork trousers and one of Da's button-downs, wrapping the familiar fabric around myself same as a hug. Then I fetch Shrunken Jim and flop onto my bed. I never realized how board-stiff my mattress was until now. Lilou's bed was practically a marshmallow compared to this.

But remembering the inside of Lilou's room brings up a whole different kind of complicated feeling. Part of me wants to pull at that feeling until it unravels, to peek at whatever is hiding underneath. But the more sensible part of me knows I can't afford to get distracted. Not when there are too many other problems I need to deal with. So I clear my throat and tell Shrunken Jim, "Okay, here's what happened."

And I explain everything. The map, the tunnel, the scales, the scientist, the witch. Shrunken Jim's bulbous eyes get wider and wider, and when I mention the witch, they almost pop out of his head completely.

Did you see her? he asks urgently. *Did she see you?*

I shrug.

Skulls and vermin, Kess. What have you gotten yourself into?

"That's just the problem," I admit. "I've got no idea."

You should've stayed in Wick's End. How many times . . . He breaks off and sighs. *Look, whatever curse Miss Starling is trying to break, it's none of your business. Leave it alone.*

"The Endling Society knows about the unnatural world, Jim. They can show us how to save the Unnatural History Museum," I say. "And I . . . I don't *want* to leave it alone. Whatever's out there is important—I know it is."

Shrunken Jim's mouth pinches tighter. *This "important" non-sense wouldn't have anything to do with a certain girl-child, would it?*

My face flushes. "I promised Lilou I'd help, that's all."

Sure. Which is why you've turned the color of a sunburned strawberry.

I tug my collar higher and turn away. So much for distracting myself with practical stuff. "Will you tell me about the Drowned World or not? No stories this time. Only facts."

He thinks about it for a long moment. Skulls and family portraits watch us silently from the shelves around my room, waiting. A branch scrapes itself across the windows like a fingernail.

Finally, Shrunken Jim huffs. *You're right about the tunnels,* he starts reluctantly. *They were made by megafauna. They do lead to the Drowned World. As far as I know, they're the only way in or out.*

My heart beats quicker. "Are there any megafauna still alive?"

Maybe, deep underground. But I'd bet the Drowned World is just a kingdom of bones nowadays. The magic down there consumes you, no matter how normal or extraordinary you are. Most of the creatures I knew were half-rotten. And that was decades ago.

Magic. A kingdom of bones. No wonder the tunnel seemed to call out to me. And perhaps that's why the scientist was so strange—perhaps he really had visited the Drowned World once.

"So why would the Endling Society go down there, if it turns you rotten?" I rub my tired eyes. "Sounds like a death trap."

Shrunken Jim clicks his tongue. *It is a death trap. But there's a golden river, remember? Humans love gold. Also, there are things . . .*

"Things?"

Things that can grant wishes. Over life, over death. He looks away, a frown etched across his greenish face. *But it's not worth the risk of meddling. Trust me. Real magic isn't like how it appears in fairy tales. It's wild and unpredictable. Wishes become curses very, very easily.*

I pull my blanket around my shoulders. I've forgotten to light my candles, and the room is darkening, washed with a murky glow from Shrunken Jim's jar.

"I wonder if the Endling Society made it to the Drowned World," I say, half to myself. "I wonder if that's why they need saving. If we need to break a curse, that could be where it came from."

Yes, well. Shrunken Jim continues to stare at the wall. *It's been seventy years. I'm not sure you can do anything about it now, whatever happened.*

Questions buzz around my head like flies. I rub at my eyes once more, wishing it all made sense. The branch taps the window again and again, and then another problem hits me. "If it's so dangerous, why would Grandpa Starling send Lilou down there?"

Did he specifically tell her to go to the Drowned World?

"No," I admit. "But the map . . ."

Maybe you're looking at this wrong. Or maybe Grandpa Starling was bonkers.

I remember his photograph, and unease creeps down my spine. None of the pieces are adding up. I still feel as though I'm missing something obvious, but I can't grab ahold of it. It settles on the tip of my tongue and vanishes just when I start to remember.

Kess? Shrunken Jim says.

"Mm-hmm?"

Promise you won't go back. If the witch really did notice you, you might not escape a second time.

"Jim," I groan. "I'm not quitting."

Yes, yes, but you don't understand what a witch really is, he says urgently. *They aren't like other unnatural creatures. They aren't born. They're made. They're what happens when a human spends too long inside the Drowned World and the human part of them gets burned away.*

"Really?" I sit up straighter. My idea of witches comes from storybooks: hunched-up crones with black hats and missing teeth. I never really considered that they might be something different.

Now imagine the kind of person who could not only find the Drowned World, but stay there for days or months or years. Imagine how dangerous they would be.

"Dangerous doesn't always mean bad."

Shrunken Jim's expression sours. *Not always. But usually.*

It sounds to me like Shrunken Jim is holding a grudge. Still, I can't help but wonder if this might connect to Grandpa Starling's instructions: *Beware the witches. Break the curse. Save the society.* Yet the more I think about it, the more my brain hurts.

I stretch upright and grab my blanket.

"Be right back," I tell Shrunken Jim. "Gotta clear my head."

And I wander until I find myself back downstairs in the Long Gallery.

Oliver is still asleep on the bench, overlooked by a display case of talismans carved from unicorn horns. He reminds me of the roaches in the bathroom, shadowed and twitchy and gross. But I wish more than anything I could ask his opinion on what to do next. Maybe we're never going to be as perfect as Lilou's family, but sometimes all I want is a hand to hold in the dark.

I toss the blanket over him and return to my room before my bare feet go numb.

11

That night, I dream of a tunnel made from glimmering golden scales. Fangs drip from the ceiling like stalactites. Someone up ahead calls my name. I try to run to them, but I can't move. When I look down, I realize I'm knee-deep in mud and it's slowly, slowly sucking me deeper and the tunnel is collapsing—

Thud. Thud. Thud.

I roll out of bed with a yelp. "What *is* that?"

Someone's at the door, Shrunken Jim says, muffled by the curtains. *I think it's your girlfriend.*

"Hush up," I snarl. My heart is still pounding, and the nightmare echoes around my head like a bad ghost. The last thing I need is for Shrunken Jim to make jokes about Lilou. "Who is it really?"

I'm serious. It's Miss Starling.

Sure enough, the clock on my nightstand reads 9:57 a.m. I've slept in again. I curse myself for forgetting to set an alarm and hurry to get dressed as quick as I can, digging around for clean socks and shirts. Not that it's much use. When I catch a glimpse of my reflection in the mirror, I look like the world's biggest mess. Bushy brown hair. Bagged eyes. Crumpled clothes.

Thud. Thud. Thud.

You aren't dressing for a party, Shrunken Jim says. *Just answer the door.*

"I thought you didn't want me to go to Eelgrass Bog?" I grumble, jamming on my glasses.

You're going anyway, he says sadly. *Might as well hurry up and stop Miss Starling from making a racket.*

So I grab my rucksack and hurry downstairs. Thanks to the snores wafting from the Long Gallery, I can guess Oliver is still asleep. Good. That's one less thing to worry about. I open the doors, and sure enough, Lilou is standing on the steps, pretty as ever. Her black hair is tied in two fresh braids, a very grown-up leather satchel is slung across her shoulders, and her lashes are lowered as she glances at her phone screen.

"Hello," I say weakly.

"Hello yourself," she says, glancing up. "Sorry if I knocked too loud. You weren't at the watch fires, so I was worried you were sick or something."

"No, I–I've just . . . um . . ."

Lilou frowns. "It's okay. I've felt strange too. That tunnel messed with my head. If you want to take the day off, that's totally fine."

"Do you want me to?" I say nervously. "Stay behind, I mean?"

She looks startled. "No. Of course I want you to come. That's maybe the only thing I *am* certain of right now. I need a friend with me."

Warmth fills me. I can't remember the last time someone my age called me their friend. *Friend.* I turn the word over in my head, memorizing every edge of how she spoke it.

I yank myself back to earth. "I definitely want to come."

Lilou grins. "Guess we better get going, then."

I grin back.

The day is overcast and chilly as we wind our way through Wick's End. Lilou's satchel bumps against her hips with each step, clattering noisily. She must catch me looking, because she explains, "I've brought different supplies today, now that we know about the tunnel. Headlamps, backup flashlights, marking chalk, knee pads, first aid kit, rope, batteries, a satellite phone, masks for the smell, and gingersnap cookies. Y'know, in case I feel sick again."

"About the tunnel," I say. "I did some, uh, research last night."

"Did you find anything?" Lilou waves brightly to another group of kids across the street. "Google betrayed me. I swear there's *nothing* online about Eelgrass Bog, except that it's . . . well, a bog."

"Remember how that scientist mentioned the Drowned World?" I say. And I try to recall everything Shrunken Jim told me about the golden river and magic and how witches are made. Hopefully it doesn't sound too strange. By the time I've finished, we're already approaching the watch fires.

"Huh," Lilou says. "Near-certain death? Should've brought more cookies."

"Are you scared?"

"Not yet. Are you?"

"No," I say. Somehow, impossibly, it's the truth. Now that we're closer to Eelgrass Bog, the excited tingling has overtaken the cobwebs inside my chest. I need to see where that tunnel ends. If the Endling Society really was involved with the fabled kingdom of bones, I'm even more certain they'll know how to find a mind-blowing new exhibit for the Unnatural History Museum. It's worth the risk.

Crossing over is easier this time. We know the mud won't immediately swallow us whole, even if it does a pretty good attempt at swallowing our boots. Toads chatter, and a cool breeze yanks at my coat, lively as a welcome. There's still a slight prickle on the back of my neck, the kind that comes from being watched. What did Shrunken Jim say? *Witches are what happens when a human spends too long inside the Drowned World and the human part of them gets burned away.*

I shiver and try to think of something else. "Lilou?"

"Mm?"

"I'm sorry for running away yesterday," I say, because the embarrassment is enough to smudge away my unease. "You, um, have an amazing family. I hope they don't hate me for being rude."

"Hate you?" Lilou laughs. "My parents are already asking when you can come around again. Dad wants to test a new tempeh taco recipe on you, though I made him promise he wouldn't put mushrooms in the tortillas this time. Don't want you getting poisoned."

"Not till after we've found the Drowned World," I joke. "Have to face the monsters first."

Lilou pulls a face and narrowly misses tripping over a tussock. "Do you—whoops!—really believe there's a hidden world underneath Eelgrass Bog?"

She doesn't make it sound ridiculous. Her voice is serious, as if there is no right or wrong answer. So I reply truthfully, "Yeah. Do you?"

"Honestly? No." Lilou yanks at a tuft of grass as she walks past and twirls it. "The universe is made of *logic*, not stories. Even Grandpa knew that. It's why he found cursed objects fascinating—because he liked figuring out the science behind what made them strange. I bet the Endling Society was the same. They probably wanted to find a reasonable explanation for those tunnels."

"Unless there isn't one."

"There must be," Lilou says fervently. "I know—I *knew* Grandpa. I would've known if he'd found a magical underworld." There's a long pause as she knots the grass around her fingertips, a frustrated frown etched across her face. "Do you think it's possible to love someone and keep gigantic secrets from them?"

"Depends on the secret," I decide. "But I'm sure your grandpa loved you."

Lilou sighs. "It's just . . . maybe I could've helped him fix whatever went wrong with the Endling Society while he was still alive, if he'd trusted me a little more. Why didn't he just speak to me instead of leaving me a pile of moldy letters and an old map?"

Our boots squelch a rhythm in the muck. I concentrate on the ground so I don't veer into a puddle.

"Well," I say as casually as I can, "we might not have met if he'd told you everything."

"True! I'm glad about *that* part," Lilou says. Am I imagining it, or are her cheeks slightly pink? She throws the grass down and adds, "Just promise you won't let me turn around this time, no matter how spooky the tunnel gets."

"Deal," I say. Deep down, I'm not sure if I'll be able to keep that promise. Not if the Drowned World really is as dangerous as Shrunken Jim said.

Except when we arrive at the tunnel, something is wrong. Through the fog, a shape has blocked the entrance. It's so massive that for a second, I think we might have found megafauna. But as we get closer, I see the truth is even more unusual.

"Is that . . . ?" Lilou gapes. "Is that a *house*?"

12

Somehow, there *is* a house where there wasn't one before. And it's easily the strangest house I've ever seen. Eight iron legs hold it above the tunnel so it appears to crouch like a mechanical spider. There's a crooked chimney, shutters with peeling lilac paint, and rainbow-glass windows. Mossy clapboard walls. A thatched roof, complete with several gray-goose nests. It doesn't move as we get closer, but the neck-pricking sensation of being watched is stronger than ever.

"Bet you a chocolate bar a witch lives here," I say. "Although, it's cuter than I'd expect, for a witch."

Lilou frowns. "How did it get here? Are those stilts *legs?*"

"I know a fairy tale about that," I say, circling the house in awe. "A witch whose hut ran about on bird legs. Mam used to read it to me all the time; I've still got the book on my shelf."

"Whatever it is, it's completely blocking the tunnel."

Lilou is right. The house is crouched low to the ground, leaving a sliver of space only big enough for a rabbit to squeeze through. I've imagined plenty of terrible obstacles we might encounter on our way to the Drowned World, but an interfering spider-house was *not* one of them.

"Suppose we could go inside," I suggest. "See if anyone's home."

Lilou raises an eyebrow. "And if it does belong to a witch?"

"We ask her politely to move her house?"

It's so ridiculous we both burst out laughing. Once we've caught our breath, Lilou says, "No, but seriously. Is it really a good idea to snoop around some stranger's house? We could always come back later. Or watch and wait."

I consider. Waiting might be smart, especially after Shrunken Jim's warnings. But this house doesn't seem sinister. It's . . . well, cute. I have a good feeling about it. And if it doesn't move, we'll never get into the tunnel.

I shrug. "Can't hurt to knock," I say, although if this is a witch's house, it almost certainly could.

Lilou clambers up the stairs before I can offer to go first, hoisting her satchel determinedly over her shoulder. I follow and try not to wobble as the house tilts. There's no bell or knocker, so Lilou raps the arch-shaped door with her knuckles.

"Hello?" she calls. "Anyone home?"

"Maybe she's gone to the grocery store," I joke.

Lilou snorts. "Either that, or she—"

The door swings open, and Lilou's words cut off.

Nobody is there. We share a glance.

"I'm pretty sure this is how ninety-nine percent of kids die in fairy tales," Lilou says. *"Don't go alone into strangers' houses* and all that."

I peer through the doorway. This house might look the opposite of scary, but a chill has settled into my bones just the same. For a second, I have the weirdest sensation of having stood on this threshold before, watching the door open by itself. But I reckon our talk of fairy tales is just reminding me of Mam's storybook.

"Well," I say cautiously, "at least we aren't alone."

"True." Lilou nods. "Do you think this means we're supposed to let ourselves in?"

"Can't hurt to look," I say. And again, I'm pretty sure it could.

Inside, everything smells of springtime and pine, as though we're in a faraway forest instead of a rotten-egg-stinking peat bog. Bunches of dried wildflowers hang from rafters: lavender, daisies, crowberries, violets, dandelions, and forget-me-nots, each tied with a black silk ribbon. They swing like clock pendulums as the house shifts.

"Hello?" Lilou calls again, stretching her fingers upward to brush the flowers as we walk deeper into the house. "Anyone?"

The house is small but crammed with *stuff*. There are tables and chairs that wouldn't look out of place in an ordinary sitting room, alongside a teetering shelf of books that have very dull titles: *A Brief History of Taxes* and *Crocheting Place Mats for Beginners*. Dozens of dirty teacups are scattered about. There's also trash everywhere: pop cans, rubber tires, giant balls of elastic bands, shoes without laces, laces without shoes. However, the closer I look, the more I notice a couple of unusual things too. There's a basket of scrolls covered in a swirly language. A case of beautifully preserved butterflies. Stacks of petrified bog wood carved into reaching hands that actually look human. And instead of being transparent, the windows are stained with pictures of angry-faced suns and eyeballs floating about like stars.

I realize my mouth is open. "Guess we could look around while we're here?"

Lilou nods, eyes wide. "It's like another museum in here."

She's right. Despite all the ordinary furniture, it does remind me of the Unnatural History Museum. Perhaps that's why it feels familiar. There are display cases here too. I spot fossils and shells nestled between the trash. There's even a complete cat skeleton propped above a menu for Gina's Hot 'n' Ready Pizza.

Then my eyes catch on a photograph half-hidden beneath a pool of hardened candle wax. It's old and worn, blurrier than any photograph I've seen before. I unpick the wax and adjust my glasses. The image shows two figures with their backs to the camera, their fingers lazily laced together like it's the most natural thing in the world.

"What's that, Kess?"

My cheeks flush. Suddenly all I can think of is holding Lilou's hand, so vividly I swear Lilou can hear me thinking it. "Oh," I mumble. "Nothing important."

"Can I see?" When she takes the photograph, an odd look crosses her face. I wonder hopefully if she's imagining the same thing as me until she says, "The boy on the left looks like Grandpa."

"Are you sure? How can you tell?"

Wordlessly, she gives it back to me. And I notice a familiar symbol scratched into the corner: a one-antlered deer skull and two crossed pens. *The Endling Society.*

That's when a person-shaped shadow falls across the room.

"You should've told me you were coming to visit," a voice says coolly. "I would have put the kettle on."

We both whirl around, a startled squeak escaping Lilou. The voice belongs to a tall woman standing stiffly by the fireplace. Her thin body is swallowed up by a humongous brocade coat the color of green glass bottles. Wavy blond hair falls thick and loose down to her hips. Her hands are covered in tatty cotton gloves. If this is the witch, then she's exactly like her house—more normal than I expected, even if she does carry the same mushroom-and-moss smell as that scientist. She's also familiar in a weird way I can't put my finger on. Especially when she steps into the light, and I realize she's much younger than I first assumed. Maybe sixteen or seventeen at most. Not a woman at all.

"You," she says, beetle-black eyes fixed on me, "shouldn't be here."

"Sorry," I whisper. A sharp pain needles my head. "We, um, we just ... Your house ... We didn't mean ..."

"But you did mean it," she interrupts. "Nobody *accidentally* crosses Eelgrass Bog. Nobody *accidentally* enters someone's house and starts rooting through their living room. It's very rude, you know."

"We know," Lilou says apologetically.

The girl whips her head around to glare at Lilou. "And who are you?"

"Lilou Starling. And this is Kess Pedrock."

"Starling?" The girl pales. "You can't be."

Lilou raises a brow at me, then clears her throat and says, "Well, I am. We're trying to follow instructions left by my grandpa. He was part of the Endling Society, and I'm pretty sure you've got a photograph of him, right here." She gestures for me to hand the photograph over, so I do.

The girl takes the photograph with trembling fingers. Her uncertain gaze flicks between Lilou, the image, and me.

"Your grandpa is Jules Starling?"

"Was," Lilou corrects sadly. Then she brightens. "Why? Did you know of him? Is that why you have his photograph?"

A shudder runs through the girl's body as though someone has stabbed a sword through her heart. She squashes her eyes closed and takes a deep, deep breath. When she reopens her eyes, she seems much older and wearier. "Yes," she whispers. "I knew Jules."

"You actually knew him?" Lilou gapes. "But that's impossible. He hasn't lived in Wick's End since he was a teenager."

"You'd have to be at least eighty years old," I point out.

The girl gives us a look that says, *And?* Then she sighs again, pacing circles around the room. Finally, she asks, "Do you drink tea?"

"Tea?" Lilou and I echo.

"You've come all this way," she grumbles. "Might as well have refreshments before I send you back to your silly little town. I harvest the ingredients myself. Eelgrass moss tea has incredible properties if you understand what you're doing. Which most people don't, because they're imbeciles."

She's rambling. Her eyes keep twitching back to me and Lilou. It makes me wonder when she last had visitors, and why she plonked her house in our path if she didn't *want* visitors, and what she knows about the Endling Society, and if any of this really makes her a witch. She doesn't seem scary enough to be a bog witch. Even if her teeth are unnaturally sharp when she chews her lip, and thin bramble tendrils are woven through her hair like they've grown from her scalp.

Soon my achy head is also heavy with questions. The strangest part is how *she* seems wary of *us*, as if we're the witches instead of her.

Lilou must be puzzling over the same questions, because she doesn't speak either as the girl flits around, grabbing pinches of this and that from old baked bean tins. I can still see the worn-out labels underneath their new tags: FOR SLEEP. FOR HEARTACHE. FOR PAIN. FOR JOY. FOR ENEMIES. FOR CALM.

The tea gets mixed into a silver teapot shaped like a curled-up rat. Three chipped mugs are placed on a tray; then finally, the girl adds a pot of boiling water from the fireplace and gestures for us to sit down. The sofa creaks worse than the Unnatural History Museum when we do.

"Here," she says shortly. "Drink up."

I sniff. My cup smells of soggy grass and mint. "What's it do?" I ask, trying not to sound too suspicious. "Is it magic?"

The girl's dark eyes flash. "Why would it be magic?"

"Well, aren't you a witch?" I say hesitantly, because I'm still not entirely sure myself. I don't mean it to be rude, but the girl clenches her jaw like I've called her a much worse name. Maybe "witch" is an insult on Eelgrass Bog. I flinch and wait for her to curse me into a cockroach.

But the girl just bites her lip with claw-sharp teeth again and mutters, "I don't use magic anymore. It's nothing but trouble."

It reminds me of Shrunken Jim's words: *Real magic isn't like how it appears in fairy tales. It's wild and unpredictable. Wishes become curses very, very easily.* I want to push further, but the girl's curt tone definitely didn't invite more questions.

I take a sip from my mug instead. It tastes exactly how it smells, and I wrinkle my nose. Needs sugar.

"My name is Ivy Holloway, by the way," the girl says. "Just Holloway will do."

"Holloway," Lilou echoes. She swallows a mouthful of her tea and immediately gags. "Um, this is . . . different."

Holloway doesn't respond.

"Can you tell us how you knew Grandpa?" Lilou tries again. "He gave me this map, see, and we think he wanted us to find something that's hidden in the tunnel beneath your house. Something to do with the Endling Society."

"And the Drowned World," I add.

Lilou passes the map to Holloway. Those three lines on the back catch the light: *Beware the witches. Break the curse. Save the society.*

Holloway barely looks at it before she hands it back. "I can't help. When you've lived as long as I have, it's difficult to remember the details of who comes and goes."

"But that photo—" Lilou tries.

"Your Endling Society came to me asking about the Drowned World, and I told them the same thing I'll tell you: stay away. If Jules ignored me and fell into trouble, that's none of my business."

Holloway speaks quickly, and I have a strong suspicion that she's lying. At the very least, she isn't telling the whole truth.

She chokes on the words "Endling Society" and "Jules" like bits of gristle and takes an extremely long gulp of tea at the end.

Lilou isn't so easily put off. "Surely you can tell us something? Even if it's just what the Endling Society was doing, or—"

"Like I said," Holloway interrupts firmly, "it's difficult to remember."

Silence falls. It reminds me of the silence that follows whenever Oliver and I argue, thick and rumbling and bitter. Lilou looks like she wants to shake Holloway upside down until all her secrets tumble out. Then, after several too-long minutes, Holloway drains the rest of her tea and slams the cup onto the tray, making both of us jump.

"Don't sulk." She huffs. "I've collected plenty of objects from the bog over the years. If you would like to search for clues about your Endling Society, be my guest."

Lilou flashes a pretty smile. "Thank you."

"I doubt you will find anything useful," Holloway adds.

"We'll try," Lilou says. She stands, and I start to follow when Holloway catches my arm. Her gloves scratch at my skin.

"Not you, Pedrock," she tells me. "You and I need to have a little chat in private."

13

"We can't split up," I blurt.

Holloway rolls her eyes. It makes her look like an actual teenager for the first time. "I'd hardly call it *splitting up*," she says. "We'll just go onto the rooftop."

"It's okay, Kess," Lilou says encouragingly. "I'll scream if anything bites."

I'm still not sure how I feel about this, but I follow Holloway into the gloomy corridor. She pulls down a ladder made from spun reeds and climbs through a hatch without bothering to make sure I'm there. The ladder tips as I scramble up, and I'm grateful Lilou can't see how wobbly I am.

But as soon as I reach the roof, I forget to be embarrassed. I forget to be cautious.

I forget everything.

Up here, I can see for miles and miles. Blackflies, geese, and a blood-red sun are poised above the horizon. Birch trees bite the sky like jagged teeth. Fog hangs close to the earth, glowing white and ghostlike. Wind knots my hair. Even though we're standing still, it feels as though we're rushing toward the distant river, faster, faster, faster. I stretch my arms out, and a delighted laugh escapes my lips.

Holloway smiles faintly from where she's leaning against the crooked chimney. Her coat and hair billow. "Not a bad view, is it?"

"It's magic!" I say. As if to prove it, a stormy cloud barges in front of the sun, and the sky shifts colors: purple, gold, orange.

"Pity the wind is misbehaving," Holloway says. "Normally autumn afternoons are more peaceful on Eelgrass Bog."

"I don't mind," I say truthfully. "It feels like the house is running."

Holloway doesn't say, *What an odd thing to mention* or *Houses can't run, Kester*. She just smiles wider, showing off her pointed teeth, and pats the space beside her. "Come sit with me."

Careful not to tumble over the edge, I wedge myself into the thatch. Straw prickles my legs, but I'm too busy gawking at the sky to care. It's so *alive*. Oliver and Shrunken Jim were wrong about Eelgrass Bog. They always made it sound gloomy, filled with creatures cut from cruel, dark things. But even Holloway isn't scary. I feel relaxed, as though I've visited before in my dreams.

I reach toward the sun. "Can we bring Lilou up here?"

"Eventually," Holloway says. "But it's you I want to speak to."

"Oh, I'm just here to help Lilou. And to find some bones for my Unnatural History Museum, although I can't seem to do *that* very well."

"I'm sure that's not true." Holloway's face twists, and I realize—I *think*—she's trying to smile. "You remind me of someone I used to know a long time ago. Someone who was extraordinarily gifted in discovering the hidden parts of Eelgrass Bog."

"Who?" I ask.

"A girl. One of the cleverest girls I've ever met."

"She doesn't sound much like me," I say. Then a strange, niggling thought occurs to me. "Was her name Ellen-Jane? My mam found entire skeletons on Eelgrass Bog when she was younger. Maybe you met her?"

Holloway gives me a long look. "Perhaps. There is a resemblance."

Warmth grows in my belly. Mam also has short, tangled brown hair and prescription glasses. There's something extra special about being compared to her, even if it does make me wish she'd told me more about her adventures on Eelgrass Bog.

"She's in Antarctica now," I say proudly. "Hired to investigate new unnatural skeletons under the ice."

I expect Holloway to look impressed. Instead, her smile fades. "You must miss her terribly."

The warmth inside me turns sharp. "Yes. But . . . her job is important. She'll come home soon."

"When?"

It's such a small question, but it makes me feel panicked, like Holloway has given me a test I've forgotten to study for. It's worse because she uses the same too-careful tone that Lilou's dads used when *they* asked about my parents. Why does everyone make it sound like Mam and Da did something wrong by leaving for Antarctica? They haven't abandoned us forever. They *haven't*.

"Soon," I repeat. "Anyway, it's fine. My brother takes care of me."

Holloway's jaw twitches with something unreadable. She

tucks a flyaway strand of bramble-hair behind her ear. "Forgive my prying," she says. "I forget that I'm not speaking to . . . Well, the details don't matter. I'm going about this the wrong way." She exhales. "Have you ever heard of heart-glow, Pedrock?"

I shake my head.

"It's a feeling that comes from inside a person. A brightness certain people possess that makes them unique. Your heart glows especially bright, Kess Pedrock."

Heat rushes up to my cheeks. I twist a strand of thatch tight around my thumb until the tip goes purple. "Pretty sure I'm not full of glow," I mutter. "Cobwebs, maybe."

Gently, Holloway touches my arm. "You underestimate yourself. Heart-glow comes from deep places. You can be angry or frightened or sorrowful and still shine bright, as long as you hold on to the things you care about. I saw it in the girl I used to know. I saw it in you, when you watched the sky. I saw it when you were with Jules Starling's granddaughter."

"Ah," I manage. It comes out as a squeak, and my cheeks grow hotter.

Holloway laughs. "I didn't mean to make you uncomfortable. I just wanted to explain what I see in you, and why I asked you up here. And why I wondered if . . . unless it's too presumptuous, but . . ."

"But?"

"Life gets rather lonely on Eelgrass Bog." Holloway clears her throat. She actually looks nervous. "Of course, we've only just met, but there's so much I could teach someone like you. Think of it like an apprenticeship. You could stay with me on Eelgrass Bog, and in return for your company, I could show you everything I know. Until your parents return," she adds hastily.

I stare at her, stunned. Whatever I expected Holloway to ask, it wasn't this.

"Could you teach me about the Drowned World?" I ask, before I can really think about what staying would mean.

She grimaces. "The Drowned World steals heart-glow. It changes who you are in the worst possible way. It is why I often use my house to guard these tunnels." Then she softens. "But there are beautiful, good secrets hidden on Eelgrass Bog too. Your mother must've known that. Now I can show them to you too."

I swallow and ask, "Why only me? What about Lilou?"

The sun reappears from behind the clouds and washes over Holloway's face. "Lilou would be missed in Wick's End."

And you wouldn't.

The words don't need to be spoken aloud; I hear them just fine. The glow inside me falters. Holloway is right. If I never came home, Oliver would probably be relieved. *He* doesn't think I'm special. *He* doesn't want to teach me things. He doesn't see me at all. But if I stayed, he'd let the Unnatural History Museum become a pest-gobbled wreck. Plus, I'd have to say goodbye to Lilou.

"I think I want to finish this expedition," I say.

"What if I promised there was nothing about the Endling Society worth finding?" Holloway says, almost desperately.

"Lilou could still come to visit. I—I could show you how to harvest moss tea."

I shake my head slowly. "It's not just that. My museum needs me. And my brother can't even make his own sandwiches, so I think he needs me too."

Holloway's shoulders slump inside her too-big green coat. She seems very human then. "Fine," she sighs.

"Another time?"

"Mmm," she says vaguely. "We should go inside now. It's getting cold." She sweeps toward the ladder, and her coat flaps around her shoulders like wings, like if she wanted, she could fly and touch the stars.

"Holloway?"

"Yes, Pedrock?"

"Maybe you could help us find bones before we go home?"

She tenses. "I'm not a bone hunter."

"Just for company," I say. Because truth is, I understand what it means to be lonely. How loneliness can ache and grow and make you feel invisible even to yourself. Perhaps there is plenty Holloway won't tell us, but I don't think she's bad. Just lost. And perhaps that's why she feels strangely familiar to me too.

"Company," she echoes. Then she almost smiles. "Why not?"

I grin back.

I follow her to the ladder and half climb, half fall back into the house. Inside, Lilou is sitting in an armchair with dozens of papers spread across her lap. Her pencil flies furiously across a pink spiral notebook. I remember what Holloway said about heart-glow—*I saw it when you were with Jules Starling's granddaughter*—and butterflies start to flap around my chest. I think again of the photograph where those Endling Society members held hands. Then I think of what it might be like to hold Lilou's hand. My cheeks flame up. Why do I suddenly feel like I've swallowed an entire garden of butterflies?

"Okay?" Lilou asks, looking up.

"Tell you later," I say quickly, because Holloway is most definitely eavesdropping, and I don't know what I want to say yet. "Did you find anything?"

Lilou rubs at her eyes and yawns. "Not really. Some photographs of plants and stuff. Notes written in French that I'll have to translate later. Oh, and this box!"

She hands it to me. It's small and dented, made from knotty wood and pearlescent inlays. I turn it upside down. It rattles—and that's when I notice the Endling Society's symbol scratched into its bottom.

"It's locked," Lilou says. "I was hoping Holloway had the key."

"Somewhere, certainly," Holloway says from behind a bookshelf. I *knew* she was eavesdropping. "You can search when we return."

"Return?" Lilou says, surprised. "From where?"

I smile. "We're going bone hunting."

14

Holloway takes us to a riverbank. Not the big river I saw from her rooftop but a smaller one, barely a trickle, bordered by rushes and abandoned goose nests. The mud here is so deep that it pours over the tops of my rubber boots. Walking is pretty much impossible, and my socks squelch unpleasantly with each step.

"You should've asked Holloway to take us into the tunnel," Lilou says, swatting at a cloud of blackflies. "We'll never get *anywhere* at this rate."

"She's really not a Drowned World fan," I say.

"No, that would be too easy," Lilou groans, then groans louder when her boot gets stuck in the mud. She yanks it free and mutters, "Now I understand why everyone believed Eelgrass Bog ate people. I swear something is chewing on my feet."

"What are you grumbling about?" Holloway calls from up ahead. I have no idea how she's managing to walk so fast. Her brocade coat is caked in brown and blackflies swarm around her face, but she actually looks . . . excited. Like we're going to the fairground instead of bone hunting in the dirt. "No better place to find unusual things than the river," she adds. "It used to be twice this size fifty years ago. As it shrinks, the most incredible objects appear."

"Like bones?" I ask.

"And buttons," she says, serious. "I found one shaped like a ladybug last month."

Lilou's lip twitches. "Sounds fantastic."

Guess that explains the clutter inside Holloway's house. Normal things must seem extraordinary to someone from Eelgrass Bog.

I adjust my glasses and begin to scan the ground, wishing I'd brought my magnification goggles. The earth is dark and soupy and thick with crawlies. Every time I think I've spotted a bone, it wriggles and worms away.

"Holloway," I say, wrenching my foot free with a *sluuurp*. "Um, have you ever actually found unnatural bones here?"

She hums. A plastic grocery bag gets untangled from a nest and shoved into her pocket. "Sometimes. Fangs and claws and whatnot. Personally, I prefer the human things that are . . ." She trails off to retrieve an empty baked bean can, eyes bright. When she tips it upside down, a waterfall of filth pours out alongside several bugs and three very, very soggy beans.

"Things that are what?" Lilou prods, wrinkling her nose.

"Connected to humans." Holloway tucks the bean can next to her plastic bag. "I haven't been able to leave Eelgrass Bog for over a hundred years, so human throwaways help me piece together the tale I'm missing."

I gape. A hundred years? No wonder she's lonely.

"Can't you sneak through the watch fires?" I ask, remembering how they flared when Shrunken Jim got too close. "Maybe if you were careful . . ."

Holloway runs her tongue along the edges of her vampire-sharp teeth. "I'd stand out too much. Besides, Eelgrass Bog is my home. We . . . belong to each other."

At least I can understand how it feels to be tied down to a place. I squat to examine a silvery object poking through the muck, hoping it's a megafauna spine—but it's just an old spoon with dented sides. Lilou digs up a matching fork. Her eyebrows are furrowed, and even with a witch standing right beside us, I'm pretty sure she's trying to puzzle out a reasonable explanation for Holloway's words.

"People don't live for more than a hundred years," she says carefully. "Especially not without getting very wrinkled and brittle. So if you *are* telling the truth . . . how did it happen?"

Holloway stiffens halfway through retrieving another plastic bag. "That is an unhappy story."

"We'd still love to hear it," Lilou says. "Wouldn't we, Kess?"

I nod. It seems kind of unfair to ask Holloway to share her life story when I've just refused her apprenticeship, especially if it's difficult for her—but I'm deadly curious to know how witches are created.

"Promise we won't tell anyone else," I say.

Holloway clutches the plastic bag tight. "There is not much to tell. Our family lived in Wick's End back when people still left offerings of milk and salt to keep the unnatural away. I had one brother and four sisters. We lived in the tiniest apartment imaginable, and every winter, I thought we would freeze to death." She shivers. "One winter, I was right. The frosts and the damp took two of my sisters within weeks of each other."

The fork slips from Lilou's fingers. She looks horrified. "Oh. I'm sorry."

"I'd heard tales of the Drowned World, of course," Holloway says dully. "I didn't care if it changed me, or if the bog ate me up. I decided anything would be better than being human, mortal and weak. So I ran away. Found a tunnel. And the rest, you already know."

"We don't!" I say. "What was the Drowned World like? Why didn't you stay down there?"

Holloway runs a muddy hand through her bramble-hair. "So inquisitive! I thought we were supposed to be bone hunting?"

"There aren't any bones," I point out.

"You have to get closer to the river, where the water moves fast." Holloway bunches up her coat and edges down the bank. She seems eager to shift away from talking about her past. "Just be careful that you don't–"

Lilou yelps.

"–trip," Holloway finishes.

Lilou must've stepped on loose ground, because she's somehow lost her footing and tumbled down the riverbank into the water. I hurry forward to help, but the ground *is* loose. One second I'm struggling to move my feet at all, and the next I'm sliding into the water as the whole riverbank gives way with a *THWAP*.

I squeak and thrash. My limbs windmill uselessly. I never

took lessons, but swimming always seemed like it would be easy, a skill people are born with. Except now my lungs are full of silty water, and weeds are wrapped around my ankles like kraken tentacles. Panic tightens my chest—

"Kess!"

Both my arms are hauled upright, Lilou on one side and Holloway on the other. As I gasp for air, it takes me a second to realize they're both laughing.

And it only takes another second to realize *why*.

"Oh," I say, coughing up a weed. Now that I'm upright, the water only reaches my elbows. The riverbed squishes beneath my feet, but there's barely any current, and if I move my arms, it's actually easier than walking along the bank. A grin spreads across my face. "That wasn't so bad."

"You're a hazard," Lilou says, but she makes it sound like a compliment.

Holloway chuckles. Her long hair hangs in clumpy, wet rat-tails. "Jules was the same. Always falling into everything. Why, when we used to search the river for bones—" She breaks off suddenly. "It doesn't matter."

But we're already on her.

"You came here with *Grandpa*?" Lilou asks.

"The Endling Society searched for *bones* here?" I say at the same time.

Holloway steps backward. "I suppose being here just reminded me of them, that's all. But it doesn't matter."

"It does," I say, fixing my glasses. "It matters to us."

She strokes her hands over the surface of the river like she's petting it, mouth pinched. "There were four members of the Endling Society. They wanted to find evidence of cursed creatures on Eelgrass Bog, so they often searched the river for old bones. Although whenever Jules was involved, nobody stayed dry—or focused—for long. They were more friends than scientists."

Lilou gives Holloway a funny look. "You came with them?"

"Sometimes." Holloway's hands move faster. "Mostly to convince them not to visit the Drowned World."

"It's really that bad, huh?" Lilou says. I still can't tell if she believes Holloway, but the lines between her eyebrows are growing deeper.

Holloway shrugs.

I kick my boots through the muddy riverbed. Plumes of brown swirl across the water. It's strange to think of the Endling Society goofing around in this same place. They've seemed kind of mysterious to me up until this point, closer to long-dead kings than a group of adventuring friends.

Holloway leans all the way back so she's floating like a starfish, her coat billowing around her. She moves her arms in lazy circles. "You know," she murmurs, "it's been ages since I shared memories out loud. It isn't *entirely* bad."

"I think you should write one of those books." Lilou flips onto her back too. "What're they called? A memoir. All about your life."

"I'd read it," I say, and lie down so I'm floating alongside Lilou and Holloway. The cold water bites at my numbed skin.

Holloway doesn't reply. But when I glance at her, she's smiling.

We float in silence for a while. The water rocks us gently, and the sky yawns above, gray and endless as an Antarctic ice shelf. The sun is low, a half grin through the fog. If I close my eyes, I can pretend I'm floating through the clouds on the back of a gigantic creature—that Lilou and Holloway and I belong to our own secret society. It's funny how . . . *right* the idea feels, even if Holloway is a prickly witch. It's a shame she can't come with us to Wick's End. I have a feeling she'd appreciate our Unnatural History Museum better than most people.

"Oi! What're you doing in my river?"

I jump at the new voice and accidentally snort a mouthful of water.

A man stands on the riverbank, glaring down at us. Baubles glitter from his clothes: fishhooks, earrings, and little vials of bog water. It's the creepy scientist from before.

"You're disturbing the specimens," he growls. "How am I s'pposed to collect algae-gobblers when you—" All the color drains from his face. His gaze locks on Holloway, and he makes a complicated gesture before spitting over his shoulder. "Witch," he says. "I *told* you children— I *warned* you—"

Holloway glares right back at him. The contented expression she'd worn before has melted away. "Go home, Dr. Stoat." Even though her eyes are hard, her tone is gentler than I'd expected.

He shrieks and makes the gesture again. "Shh! Don't speak my name!"

Holloway looks like she wants to say something else, but the man is already gone, running off into the fog with a clatter of belts and buckles. I realize my mouth is open and quickly shut it.

"That," Holloway says, "is why humans should never mix with the Drowned World. Dr. Stoat tried to find the end of the tunnel once. Only once. And now he can't tell the difference between minutes and years. He's too full of curse-touched nightmares for the watch fires to let him leave."

"He was rude." Lilou crosses her arms. "Just because you live on Eelgrass Bog, doesn't mean—"

"No, he was right. Witches are unlucky," Holloway interrupts. She pivots and climbs out of the river, using a nearby bush for balance. "They've got too much unnatural magic to have any kindness left, and their only purpose is to trick foolish travelers into staying underground until they've forgotten their own names." She huffs. "The Drowned World devours people with promises, not teeth. It collects anyone who is curious, broken, or stupid enough to search for magic and never lets them go. Perhaps that answers some of your questions."

She wrings out her hair and, without waiting for us to follow, storms away toward her spider-legged house.

Once we're all back inside, Holloway builds a fire in the hearth and tosses a fistful of tea leaves—FOR WARMTH—into the flames. They burn dark pink and immediately warm me through, chasing the wet from my clothes within minutes. The whole house starts to smell of raspberries. Holloway gets straight to work emptying plastic bags, candy wrappers, and tin cans from her pockets; no bones, of course. I've only managed to collect a fancy-looking snail shell.

To tell the truth, I'm a little spooked by everything that's happened. There's something about how everyone is treading around the Endling Society and the Drowned World that feels . . . well, darker than I expected. Like maybe Lilou and I could end up the same as Dr. Stoat, bog ridden and plagued by nightmares, unable to go home. But I also know that uncovering the secrets of the Endling Society is the best way for me to save my Unnatural History Museum. All the stories we've been told are snippets of something bigger, something important. I *know* we're on the right track, even if it's a murky one. And I'm not the kind of person who's turned around by a spot of darkness.

We'll find the Endling Society. We'll save the museum.

I *know* it.

I chew up my unease and swallow it like a spoonful of porridge. Holloway has barely spoken since we left the river, though I catch her muttering to herself under her breath as she puts her newfound throwaways into drawers. The incident with Dr. Stoat must've rattled her too. There are so many more questions I want to ask, especially about witches and megafauna and the girl who might've been my mother, but I decide it's best not to push her *too* far today.

I wrap a blanket around my shoulders and go to sit with Lilou, who's crouched by the fireplace. Pink flames crackle and cast rosy shadows over her face, as though she's got a permanent blush.

"I don't think Holloway's gonna let us into the tunnel," I say softly, pulling the blanket over my knees.

Lilou has retrieved the box she was trying to open earlier, the one with the Endling Society's crest, and is jimmying the lock with a bobby pin. "Do you think she has a point? About staying away from the tunnel, I mean? If it really is as dangerous as she says . . ."

I shift uncomfortably. "Maybe."

"Personally, I haven't ruled out poisonous gases," Lilou says. "Maybe there's something down there that makes people hallucinate. Or believe they're hundred-year-old witches."

"She *did* know your grandpa," I point out. "How d'you explain that if she isn't a witch?"

"I don't know," Lilou admits brightly, "but I'm going to find out. No evidence for witchcraft yet."

"What if the Endling Society visited the Drowned World?" I wonder aloud. "What if they got cursed to be witches too, and that's why they need saving?"

Lilou twists the bobby pin, tongue poked out in concentration. "*Or* they also breathed poison gas. Otherwise Grandpa would've—aha!"

The lid pops open. We both lurch forward to riffle through the contents. At first I'm eager, hoping for golden bones or notebooks telling us exactly how curses work, but my eagerness quickly fades into disappointment. It's just . . .

trash. Photographs of ordinary plants. Blank notepaper. A woolen sock that smells worse than Shrunken Jim. And rattling around in the corner, a crooked little key.

"Maybe they used invisible ink." Lilou squints at the notepaper.

But I'm more focused on the key. My pulse quickens. Because the longer I stare, the more I realize that it isn't trash at all. I know this key.

And I know exactly what kind of door it unlocks.

15

"The Unnatural History Museum," I realize. "This is a key from the Unnatural History Museum!"

Lilou's eyes widen. "Really?"

I nod. "I'm in charge of keys for cleaning. This is definitely one of ours."

"Oh, Kess, this is brilliant!" Lilou cries. "D'you realize what this might mean? The Endling Society is even more connected to your museum than we thought! And now we have a lead that *doesn't* involve sneaking into the Drowned World!"

"What are you shouting about?" Holloway asks, circling around the clutter to stand behind us. When she notices the key, her whole body stiffens. "What is that?"

Lilou flashes her braces. "We found an Unnatural History Museum key in your box. Could we borrow it, please?"

Holloway looks at the key as though it has insulted her worse than Dr. Stoat. Her mouth tugs downward. "That may not be a good idea. Haven't I already explained the dangers of meddling in things you don't understand?"

"It isn't *really* meddling," Lilou says. "And technically the key belongs to Kess, if it's from her museum. We'll bring it back once we've used it, promise."

"But . . . I doubt it's important," Holloway says feebly. "That box is full of inconsequential objects the Endling Society left behind."

"We won't know until we bring it to the museum," I point out. "Please?"

Holloway hesitates. I can almost hear her scrambling for a reason to say no—which means the key *must* be important. Otherwise, why would she care? Then she exhales sharply and says, "Fine. You are right. If it is an Unnatural History Museum key, then it belongs to Kess."

"Thank you." I close my fingers tight around the key's edges.

"Yes," Lilou says, "thank you."

Holloway grunts.

"Maybe we could visit again and tell you what it unlocks," I say hesitantly, because I don't want to end our visit on a sour note. "We could go bone hunting in the river again."

A light sparks in Holloway's eyes. But it's blown out almost immediately and replaced with something tired and cold. "You should both stay in Wick's End. Eelgrass Bog is no place for two little girls. I'll return you home now."

She whirls away before we can argue. Lilou and I share a *that was weird* glance. I shrug, then look again at the key in my palm. Who did it belong to? Lilou's grandpa? Or one of the other members? Whatever the case, a flicker of excitement glows in my heart. I *knew* the Unnatural History Museum was connected to the Endling Society. I *knew* the puzzle pieces fit together somehow.

I'm so preoccupied with possibilities, it takes me a moment to realize the house is moving.

In fact, it's *walking*.

The flowers on the rafters swish from side to side, and a sloppy *thruck-THRUCK* fills my ears as the stilts plunge in and out of the mud. Lilou and I share another an incredulous glance. When Holloway offered to return us home, I didn't figure she meant it literally.

"Magic?" I say, hopeful.

"Mechanics," Holloway says. "I don't mess around with magic, remember?"

That's less interesting in my opinion, but Lilou brightens. "You can steer it like a ship," she breathes. "Those levers by the fireplace . . . they control the direction of the stilts, don't they?"

Holloway just smiles thinly and keeps her hands on the knobs. The light turns her blond hair into a swirl of different colors as it beams through the stained-glass windows. The faster the house moves, the more it feels like we're trapped inside a giant kaleidoscope.

Thruck-THRUCK, thruck-THRUCK, thruck-THRUCK.

It doesn't take long to reach Wick's End, even though the tunnel was at least an hour's walk from town. Holloway yanks the levers, and the house comes to an abrupt halt. Lilou and I both trip forward.

"Here," Holloway says tonelessly.

"Thank you," I say. "For, um, everything."

Her shoulders twitch in the ghost of a shrug. Lilou gathers her satchel and heads for the door. I follow quickly after. But just as I'm about to cross the threshold, Holloway grabs ahold of my arm.

"Be careful, Kess Pedrock," she says in a low voice. "I meant what I said about meddling. It's dangerous to dig for secrets. You might not like what you find."

"There's nothing bad in the Unnatural History Museum," I tell her. "Well. Except for Oliver."

Holloway darkens. She takes a breath like she's about to say something important, something heavy and creeping—but instead she turns away.

"Just be careful," she says. "And whatever you find, stay away from the Drowned World."

We've been dropped about a quarter of a mile outside the watch fires. The afternoon sky is orange with smoke, and our footsteps squelch in time with the cricket songs. I twiddle the key in my pocket, my mind a million miles away.

Your heart glows especially bright, Kess Pedrock.

"If we keep doing this, we have to build a footpath," Lilou grumbles, yanking her foot free from the muck. "Urgh, honestly!"

The Drowned World devours people with promises, not teeth.

Lilou nudges me with her elbow. "Oh, I almost forgot to ask! What did Holloway tell you when you went up to the rooftop?"

"She just . . ." I flush. "It wasn't important. I think she mostly wanted to show off the view."

I wait for Lilou to question me. But she just shrugs and says, "I bet you could see everything from the rooftop. At least that's something."

Distantly I'm aware of Lilou continuing to chat to me, something about her dads' curfew rules, but I can't focus except to nod every few minutes. I barely realize we've crossed the watch fires until the Unnatural History Museum appears.

It's a mess. Ivy gobbles at the pathway, snarling up the gate and twisting itself around the long-broken mailbox. The boxwood hedge reaches toward what's left of Mam's garden. Holes scatter across the rooftop. Maybe I never noticed, but I swear there are cracks in the windows that weren't there earlier.

"This is me," I say very unnecessarily.

"I'll come by as soon as I can. Tomorrow we can figure out what that key unlocks."

"Bet it's a whole room of world-serpent scales."

"Or a book of secret code."

"Or maps of the Drowned World."

"Or vials of monster poison."

I let myself grin. "If it's a secret room, it must be hidden well. Otherwise I would've already found it."

"Grandpa *was* sneaky," Lilou says fondly. Then: "You'll wait for me, right? No searching without me? I know it's your museum, but—"

I cross my heart. "Promise."

She beams. "Tomorrow, then." She skips off with her muddy satchel like we had a kids' playdate in my backyard instead of a trek across Eelgrass Bog. I watch her go, heart flutter-beating like I really do have a glow inside my chest.

My mind is still whirring with possibilities of secret doors as I approach the front steps, hardly registering the new *Wick's*

End Daily newspaper scattered everywhere. It's amazing how things can feel so wrong and so perfect at the same time. I shake my head. What I really need is sleep—

Bony hands grab my collar and slam me against the wall. Air whooshes out of my lungs.

"Where have you been?" Oliver hisses.

As usual, he looks absolutely terrible. Cobwebs form sticky clusters in his unkempt hair. His wire-rimmed glasses are bent sideways across his nose. His clothes are rumpled and sour smelling, and his eyes are bloodshot. I've never seen him so angry. But angry or not, he's awake again, and I can't help but feel a rush of relief. Then I shove him away. He almost falls over.

"None of your business," I snap, tugging my coat straight again. "Vermin, Ollie. Keep your socks on."

He glares daggers at me. "It *is* my business. Mam and Da put me in charge for a reason. I know you've been up to no good. I saw that box with the bird skeleton."

It takes a second for my brain to rewind. So much has happened since Lilou gave me that box.

"A friend gave it to me," I say coolly.

Oliver goes rigid. "What friend?"

"Why did you break it?"

"I think it's . . . stolen." He coughs. "What would Mam and Da think, Kester? Hiding stolen boxes? Running away? Coming back dragging half the mud from Eelgrass Bog with you?"

"They'd be prouder of me than you," I shoot back, hoping it hurts. Hoping it's true. "Besides, that box *wasn't* stolen."

"Then who gave it to you?"

I fold my arms and keep silent.

Oliver sighs. "Fine. Whatever. You're grounded."

"Grounded?" I splutter.

He shrugs. "Should've done it earlier, really. It's impossible for me to concentrate when you're determined to be a gigantic nuisance. No more leaving the museum until I say so. Actually, no more leaving your *room*. No visitors. No friends. Play pretend with your pickled head if you're bored."

Cold stabs my stomach. "You can't," I say. "Ollie, the museum—"

"I've got it, all right? Just go to your room and stay there."

He says it in such a snooty, fake grown-up way, I might've laughed if he wasn't trying to ground me in the middle of my expedition. How can he really think I'm the problem?

"You can't ground me," I snap.

"Actually, I can. Mam and Da put me in charge—"

"But you *aren't* Mam or Da! Vermin, I wish *you'd* gone to Antarctica instead of them!"

Oliver recoils, but I don't feel sorry. Not one bit. My anger stretches like a scream, and I push past him before I say something worse.

"Kester! Kester, get back here—" Oliver doubles over, clutching the edge of a display cabinet as though he's about to pass out. My concern flares up again. But if he needed my help, he'd ask for it. I've got bigger things to worry about.

I take the stairs two at a time, up to my attic bedroom. The door slams behind me.

Hark who's still alive, Shrunken Jim says. *Did you find the Drowned World?*

"Nope," I say, peeling off my coat and kicking it under my bed. "Got blocked by a witch. Well. Half witch."

Half? Shrunken Jim's eyebrow-stitches rise in astonishment. *What . . . what makes a half witch?*

"She's really old, but she only looks sixteen. She doesn't like magic. And her house can walk, but apparently that's mechanics." I wipe down my glasses with a clean kerchief. "She wasn't evil like you said."

I never said evil, Shrunken Jim grumbles. *I said dangerous.*

"Plus, she gave us this." I hold out the key. "It's an Unnatural History Museum key, but it belonged to the Endling Society. They were connected somehow."

Throw it away, Shrunken Jim suggests. *Witches don't help people out of kindness. They're compulsive bargainers. What did she make you promise in return?*

"Nothing," I say.

She probably let you go because it unlocks something terrible.

"Drama queen."

Pragmatist.

"I don't know what that means," I huff. "If Holloway wanted to hurt us, she could've poisoned our tea. Or trampled us with her house. Or pushed me off the roof. Or—"

Okay, okay, he grumbles.

Anyway, the key belongs to the museum. It can't be bad. It feels like possibility and mystery and Lilou's smile when she realized we had a new lead. I can't explain it to Shrunken Jim. I just know I want to hold on to the light wherever I can.

All of the spare Unnatural History Museum keys are

kept in an old chocolate cookie tin underneath my dresser. I stretch down on my knees and pull it out. The lid clicks off with enough dust to make my eyes water. Dozens of keys pour across the floorboards, most of them near identical to the one from Holloway's house.

Looks like a door key, Shrunken Jim says, peering with his bulbous eyes.

I nod in agreement. The smaller keys unlock display cabinets. This one is definitely closer to a door key, which is weird, because I can't think of any doors I haven't opened before.

"Do we have any hidden doors, Jim? Behind an exhibit or something?"

Not that I can remember. Perhaps the Endling Society kept extra copies of the front door keys.

I scowl. "You have no imagination."

Most keys in the cookie tin are labeled in Mam's teeny-tiny handwriting, with tags tied onto their handles. *Third-floor bathroom. Cellar. Skeleton gallery closet. Kitchen. Kess's bedroom.* If you laid them out, you could create a pretty good map of the museum. Except a room is missing.

The library.

Oliver's library.

He keeps the main key for himself so I can't interrupt his very important moping; but I never thought to check for a spare before.

"If you had a secret," I say, "a library might be a clever place to hide it, right? With all those shelves and books?"

Suppose so, Shrunken Jim says absently.

My brain churns. Of course, there might be nothing there. Just because Holloway found the key in a mishmash of abandoned things doesn't mean it unlocks a secret. But there's a chill oozing across my skin all the same.

It's dangerous to dig for secrets. You might not like what you find.

I know I promised Lilou I'd wait for her before exploring, but if I wait until tomorrow, Oliver will have locked himself inside again. And if I'm grounded, Lilou won't be allowed to search with me. This isn't a time for museum-mouse Kess. I have to check. Tonight.

What? Shrunken Jim demands. *What's that look?*

"We're sneaking into the library," I say determinedly. "Soon as Oliver is asleep."

To my surprise, Shrunken Jim doesn't look thrilled by the idea of going behind Oliver's back. If anything, his green skin has paled. *Kess,* he says. *Maybe you shouldn't.*

"Why not?" I frown.

Because . . . His forehead wrinkles. *I just have a bad feeling.*

I pat the lid of his jar. "Don't worry, Jim. We won't get caught."

He doesn't answer, eyebrow-stitches drawn close together.

There's nothing left to do but wait. I heave a ginormous book about cave paintings from my shelf, light a candle, unwrap a chocolate bar, and curl up on my window ledge to wait. My clock ticks. Ticks. Ticks.

Finally, when my eyelids are iron heavy, I hear a door shut downstairs. Then the *creak-creak* of slow footsteps on the staircase. I hold my breath. Maybe, just maybe, Oliver will knock on my door and apologize. We'll hug, despite his stench. I'll graciously forgive him, and he'll notice my favorite photograph of our family in Maine. *Doesn't that seem forever ago?* he'll say. *We should get ice cream together soon, before we forget what it tastes like—*

A second door clicks open and closed.

"He's in his bedroom," I whisper, both disappointed and relieved.

Ready for takeoff, Shrunken Jim says, sounding resigned.

I unwind myself from the ledge, slip Holloway's key into my pocket, and gather up my candle and Shrunken Jim. Quiet as possible, I tiptoe into the hallway.

Everything is dead and still. The only other living creatures around are a nest of silverfish in the woodwork. Even the ivy hanging across the windows is lifeless. As I move through the exhibits, I keep my eyes peeled for hidden doors. But there's nothing I haven't noticed before. *This* house doesn't change. Not the Skeleton Gallery, not the Hall of Curses, not the Terrarium, not the fireplaces, and not the staircases. Still, something is . . . off. Like the whole Unnatural History Museum is holding its breath, waiting.

Straight ahead, Shrunken Jim mutters.

"Shh. I know where the library is."

Just checking. That's a very tiny candle, and humans have such pathetic eyeballs.

"At least they're not pickled," I say, fishing out the key.

Ouch.

Every bone in my body shivers, as though I am made of spiders and restless things. I've never felt nervous about visiting any part of the museum before. But the library has been capital-*F* Forbidden since my parents left. Deep down, I don't want Oliver to get even angrier at me. And I don't want to discover that he's kept secrets either.

I suck in a lungful of dusty air and calm my thoughts. Then I step, step, step, until the door is close enough to touch. With a shaky hand, I slip Holloway's key into the lock.

It fits.

And with a *click*, the library door opens.

16

For the first time since I can remember, I walk into my parents' library. There are no alarms or booby traps. Oliver doesn't come running through the entranceway. Even Shrunken Jim is silent.

To say the library is a mess would be like calling the ocean a puddle. There's paper *everywhere*. I can't see a speck of furniture that isn't covered by clutter. Stacks of notebooks taller than me teeter like a leather-bound forest. Mam's desk, once neatly organized, is drowned under layers of charts. Hundreds upon hundreds of copies of the *Wick's End Daily* newspaper form larger towers—some even cover the walls, oozing out of cracks between the bookshelves.

"How are we supposed to find anything in here?" I say, astonished. "He mustn't throw anything away *ever*."

Shrunken Jim's eyes are more bulbous than usual. Except for some reason, he's watching me instead of the library. *Guess we know where the paper-roaches have been feasting,* he says cautiously.

Unease trickles down my spine. I should have waited for Lilou. I should tiptoe back to bed, then make a proper plan with her tomorrow.

Except I can't walk away.

Without really meaning to, I move toward the desk. Most of the charts look like strange calendars. Oliver has written in the margins, but his handwriting is too scrawly for me to read. I spot an open notebook that seems to be a diary. The entries are short and also in Oliver's impossible handwriting. If this is what he meant by "paperwork," it doesn't look very official.

"This is worse than bone hunting," I mutter. There's so much to search through, and I don't even know what to search *for*. "Can you watch the door in case he wakes up, Jim?"

Shrunken Jim sighs. *Sentry duty. My favorite.*

I set down my candle and weave through the book forest, glancing at the newspapers pinned on the wall. The front-page headlines seem too ordinary to be worth keeping: MIDDLE SCHOOL ART SHOW ENDS IN DISASTER. MAYOR ADOPTS NEW TURTLE. BIRDHOUSE CLUB ANNOUNCES END TO FIERCE LEADERSHIP BATTLE. The newspapers get older as I move around, starting with last week and drifting backward into last year, and the year before that.

"Vermin." I shiver. "How far back do these things go?"

Two years. Five years. Ten years. Twenty years. Fifty years. My heart beats against my rib cage when I see a date from seventy years ago. Why does Oliver have newspapers from the time of the Endling Society?

I have to crouch to see what must be the oldest newspaper. It's folded into a corner between bookshelves, yellowed with age and crumpled like it has been read many times before. The front-page picture is of a black-and-white steamship leaving a crowded harbor: TRAGEDY IN SOUTH: 67 LIVES LOST AS RESEARCH VESSEL SINKS EN ROUTE TO STOWELL BASE, ANTARCTICA.

My gut wrenches. Stowell Base is where Mam and Da are stationed. It's a coincidence, of course; this ship sank seventy years before my parents made their journey. But sadness floods through me just the same. I can't help but imagine a boat full of people sinking into a dark, frozen ocean, thousands of miles away from home.

It's a lonely thought and makes my arms ache to hug my parents again. It's times like these that it hits me how far away Antarctica really is, and it feels as though Mam and Da have fallen off the edge of the world, beyond anywhere I'll be able to reach. Which is silly, because I *have* been able to reach them. I've written them letters and they–they–

Have they ever written back?

My heart beats, beats, beats. I can't remember. I can't *remember*.

Want to take a break? Shrunken Jim asks anxiously.

"No," I manage to say, folding the newspaper back into place. I can't let myself get shaken by a tragedy that happened before any of us were even born.

Holloway's voice floats back into my head: *It's dangerous to dig for secrets.*

I kick down the coldness stretching under my skin and search through Oliver's drawers. Reference books. Unwashed forks shoved underneath pencil trays. No wonder we are always running out of cutlery. I find dozens of calendars, newspaper clippings, books, and word-heavy diaries, but no sign of the Endling Society.

Until I notice a large redwood box on the top of a shelf. The lid is etched with a one-antlered deer skull and two crossed pens–same as the box in Holloway's house. This one is just bigger.

Carefully, I climb onto a chair and lift the box down, almost tumbling sideways from the weight. Doesn't help that I'm trembling like a leaf in a polar blizzard.

"Stuck," I mutter, pulling at the lid.

I pause. I should wait for Lilou, then we could open it together.

Tick-tock, Kess, Shrunken Jim says, suddenly alert. *I can hear something upstairs. Maybe we should go now.*

Vermin. This box is too heavy to lift quickly. Heart hammering, I tug at the lid until something splinters and one of the hinges breaks loose. I force it open. Inside there are more notebooks, charts, and photographs. With a beat of surprise, I recognize a photo of my parents. My throat closes with longing. There's us at a carnival. Shopping at a new mall. Camping in the woods. At home in the museum. Me and Oliver and Mam and Da. My heart clenches, and tears pour down my cheeks hot and fast. I miss them so much it hurts.

Oh, Kess, Shrunken Jim says.

"Fine." I shake my head. "Just—it's silly—"

Crying isn't silly.

I sniff and shake my head again. I try to stay focused, but there's an aching, dark thing inside my stomach, growing bigger and bigger every time I turn over another photograph. The sadness I felt after reading that newspaper headline has started to grow teeth.

And then I flip a photograph that's . . . different from the others.

I rub leftover tears from my eyes. It's filmier than the rest. More crumpled. It shows a teenage girl with long, wavy blond hair and an oversized brocade coat. Clawed fingernails. Night-dark eyes.

Why do we have a picture of Holloway?

The next photograph is almost identical to the one we found in her house. Two people, hands knitted together. This time they're facing the camera. And it's clear enough to make out their faces. Lilou was right. The boy on the left *is* her grandpa, also a teenager. I'd recognize his too-pretty face anywhere.

He's holding *Holloway's* hand.

"What?" I choke out. She said she barely knew the Endling Society. So how come she's grinning at Lilou's grandpa like he's the center of the universe?

Underneath, a caption reads *Jules & Ivy, April 1955.*

I feel sick. A spinning, dizzy kind of sick.

Because I know that handwriting. It's the same barely readable handwriting I found moments ago in the diary. It's the same handwriting that covers all the papers littered around the library.

It's dangerous to dig for secrets.

My trembling hands move by themselves. I turn over another photograph of Jules and Holloway laughing together, balancing on an old log. Another of them digging. And then another that includes a third figure. A thin boy with wire-rimmed glasses and a sallow face, sticking his tongue out at the camera, his arms full of books.

It's Oliver.

The dark, aching thing inside me shrieks. Blood pounds in my ears, and I have to double over to stop myself from throwing up.

Kess! Shrunken Jim cries. *Kess, what did you find?*

I can't answer. It's too big. Too much. Too impossible.

I force myself to turn over the final photograph. Somehow I already know what I'm going to see. And sure enough, there's a fourth figure in the mix. A stout twelve-year-old girl with round glasses and short, bushy hair, holding a rat skull. She's sadder than I remember, a deep-hurt kind of sad. She stands tucked between Jules Starling and Holloway with the ghost of a smile on her lips, eyes flicked to Oliver, who is pulling a silly face.

She's me.

The caption reads *Oliver & Kess & Ivy & Jules, March 1955. AKA The Endling Society.*

I scream.

17

I scream and scream and scream. I scream my throat raw, until it feels like my lungs might explode, and it's still not enough.

Kess! Shrunken Jim cries. *He'll hear you!*

Sure enough, the library door slams open, and Oliver stumbles through in his threadbare pajamas. He looks angry until he notices the photographs. Then he just looks horrified.

I hardly register his presence. Because the dates on those photos—

And that sunken ship—

My parents—

"Not again," Oliver chokes out. "Listen, Kester, I can explain."

"Explain *what?*" My voice cracks wide open. "This doesn't make sense. It can't—*we* can't be the Endling Society."

Oliver stays silent. He's staring at the photographs like they're ghosts, the worst ghosts to ever haunt the planet. I don't wait for him to find his tongue. I just grab the photographs and Shrunken Jim and run past Oliver, barefoot, out of the library and out of the Unnatural History Museum and into the night.

I have to find Lilou. If anyone can make everything feel okay, it's her.

"*Kess!*" Oliver shouts, stumbling after me. "Kester, please come back!"

I run faster. Faster. Faster. Fast enough that the wind blows away my tears. My bones ache and my brain hurts.

"Kester! Stop!"

Past the Mulberry Tree. Past the grocery store. I skid around a corner. Run, run, run. The pavement is rough and slippery, and a couple of late-night cars beep their horns at me. My feet burn. By the time I see Lilou's driveway I'm pretty sure my soles are bleeding. I can't hear Oliver behind me anymore.

The lights are on in Lilou's house; her dads are watching television in the front room with the curtains open. So I swerve off the front path and go straight to Lilou's bedroom window.

"Lilou!" I whisper-cry, banging on the glass. "*Lilou!*"

Curtains swish back. Lilou pokes her head out, jaw dropping at the sight of me. "Kess? Oh my gosh, what—"

I try to say something to explain, but my head is full of icebergs and sunken ships and a terrible deep-punch grief that just about pulls me apart. I swallow another scream. My knees buckle.

"Oh, Kess. What's wrong?" Lilou wriggles over the windowsill to crouch beside me. "Are you hurt?"

I can't find the words. Can't explain what I don't understand. I wrap my arms around my middle like that'll stop me from cracking open, and I sob and sob. Lilou pulls me close to her chest. Her pajamas smell like sugar cookies. She doesn't ask any more questions. Just hugs me tight.

"It's okay," she whispers. "Shh, it's okay."

It isn't.

I hate Oliver. I hate Holloway for giving me that key when she must've known what it unlocked. I hate both of them for lying. I hate myself for not remembering how any of this could make sense. But I can't do anything except cry harder than I've ever cried before. Lilou hugs me tighter.

"It's okay," she repeats softly. "Breathe. It's okay."

But it isn't.

It isn't.

It isn't.

18

When my tears dry up and my heartbeat calms down, Lilou helps me through the window into her room, leaves for a minute, then returns with two mugs of hot chocolate. One gets pushed into my hands; it's the proper frothy-marshmallow kind. I breathe slowly, in and out, and lean into her ginormous stack of purple pillows. Lilou sits cross-legged on the other end of her bed, frowning at the photographs I brought. Occasionally she frowns at Shrunken Jim too.

"Are you angry?" I say quietly.

She looks surprised. "Why would I be angry?"

"Because I should've waited for you to use the key."

"Pfft. That hardly matters anymore," she says. Frowning, she holds up the photograph of me, her grandpa, Oliver, and Holloway. "*This*, however, doesn't make sense."

I stare into my hot chocolate. "I know."

"You'd have to be eighty-one years old."

"I know."

"Your brother would be eighty-four."

"I know."

"But Grandpa was an old man. Like, a real one."

"I know."

Lilou runs a weary hand over her hair. She's only wearing one braid tonight, and it's messy, tied with a tiger-print scrunchie. "Have you considered . . . maybe these pictures are fake?"

I shake my head. Seeing those pictures didn't feel like seeing something new. It felt like tripping over a very old memory. It's the same as when I first visited Eelgrass Bog and saw Jules Starling's face and Holloway's house. Except now I know why they were so oddly familiar. Because I *had* seen them before.

"They're real," I say dully.

"And you have no idea what happened?"

I hug a pillow close. Lilou's whole room is soft and warm, with its plastic glow-in-the-dark stars, gauzy curtains, and stuffed animals. The lampshade with stenciled ballerinas radiates soft pink. Every corner seems to whisper, *It's okay, it's okay.*

"No," I admit. "I—I can't remember anything. We were a regular family before my parents left, but that . . ."

"Must've been seventy years ago," Lilou finishes. She laughs without humor. "Wow, this is bizarre. All this time, I had an actual member of the Endling Society with me. *You* were who Grandpa wanted me to save."

"But save *how*?"

"I'm not sure yet," she admits, reaching to hold my hand. "But there's gotta be a reason why you haven't aged and why you can't remember anything. We'll get to the bottom of it. Even unnatural things must have logic."

I focus on the warmth of Lilou's hands curled around mine. The way the marshmallows are turning goopy in my cup. Grandpa Starling wanted her to save me? Could that be true? Deep down, I've always known something was not right. The brain cobwebs. The forgetting. The way everything outside the Unnatural History Museum felt extra loud and bright, the too-new devices I didn't understand. The way I missed my parents with the kind of heart-bruising ache that comes with realizing something beloved was gone forever.

I choke on a sob.

"Sorry," I sniff. Fresh tears pour down my cheeks.

"Don't you dare apologize." Lilou swaps my hot chocolate for a box of tissues, draping an arm around my shoulder so we're pressed close together. We sit silently and watch shadow-ballerinas from the lampshade twirl across the walls. I lean into her. Her pajamas are soft against my skin, her fingers still twined with mine.

"My parents are dead, Lilou," I whisper through my tears. "They aren't coming back."

She props her head on top of mine. This time she doesn't tell me it's okay. Just waits for me to speak again.

"If the Endling Society . . . if *we* really did go down to the Drowned World, maybe that's why we're . . ."

Cursed, Shrunken Jim says flatly. He's kept quiet since we left the museum, as though the news has shaken him too. But the way he says "cursed" fills me with cold, hollow dread. It reminds me of Holloway's words about the

Drowned World: *It changes who you are in the worst possible way.*

"Don't worry about that now," Lilou says. "One thing at a time, yeah?"

"Yeah," I echo, wiping my nose with a tissue.

"And I'll be here, no matter how long it takes to figure everything out. No matter how weird it gets." She shifts so we're facing each other, faces inches apart. Her deep brown eyes are shiny, like she's trying not to cry too. "I know I kept searching for natural explanations for unnatural things, but it's only because . . . well, it's less scary to pretend you understand the world, right?"

Despite it all, relief melts through me. "You really believe me?"

She gives a watery laugh. "How can I not? I didn't think witches and curses were possible before I met you, but these photographs are pretty hard evidence. To tell the truth, I think I've been ignoring other evidence for a long time. But I promise—"

A knock sounds at the door, cutting Lilou off. Andres Starling's voice leaks through the cracks. "Why is your light still on? Are you talking to someone? It's late, kiddo."

Lilou flushes. One hand stays clenched around mine. "Sorry, Dad! Just . . . um, video-calling Sumi about her . . . hamster."

There's a long pause.

"Finish up," Andres says eventually. "I don't want to deal with the tired-grumpy-beast version of you tomorrow."

Lilou winces and blushes pinker. "Sure. G'night."

"Good night, Lils."

The floor creaks as Andres's footsteps trail away. Lilou

releases an enormous sigh. "Honestly. Does he think I'm still ten years old?"

I smile weakly. It's not Lilou's fault, but now I'm back to thinking about how crumpled-up my family is compared to the Starlings. My parents won't ever check on me again. Oliver certainly doesn't care if I'm tired in the mornings. And the more I think about it, the more I realize that he must've known the truth about our parents. He promised he was mailing my letters. He told me they were coming home. That means he kept me in the dark for seven whole decades. I'm not sure I'll ever forgive him for that. I can't trust him to tell me the truth, and Jules Starling is dead, which means the only person who might have answers is—

Holloway.

"What is it?" Lilou mutters, like she can hear my thoughts.

"We need to go back to Holloway's house," I say. "She was part of the Endling Society too. She can explain what's wrong."

Lilou looks unconvinced. A shadow-ballerina leaps across her face. "Are you sure? She hid the truth last time."

"She must've had a reason," I say determinedly, getting off the bed. "It's not like we can believe anything Oliver tells us."

"Can't we?"

I stiffen. "He's lied about my family and the Endling Society for *seventy years*. I don't want to talk to him."

Lilou nods and grabs a satchel from under her bed. "We can sneak back out through the window. If we're home by morning, my dads won't ever know we were gone."

The burble of the television suddenly switches off. A light clicks. And Lilou doesn't hesitate. She passes me a pair of sneakers, then yanks on her own boots, tosses her satchel over her shoulders, and slips out the window. I grab Shrunken Jim and cram the Endling Society photographs into my pockets. No turning back until I've found answers. I follow Lilou through her window. Shrunken Jim yelps. But it doesn't hurt, aside from a small jolt in my knees, and I'm on my feet again in moments.

"Okay," I say to Lilou, breathless. "Now what?"

Lilou is already running. "This way!"

We duck through a garden gate and into a litter-strewn alleyway. The night is cold and dark and biting. I feel like a shadow flitting across the streets, not quite real around the edges. But when the panic starts to squash my throat again and my feet stumble, Lilou reaches out to clutch my hand.

"Almost there," she pants.

"Are you . . . are you sure about this?" I pant back. "You can . . . you can still go home. Going to Eelgrass Bog at night . . . it'll be . . ."

"Dangerous," Lilou finishes. "But Grandpa wanted me to help finish this, and I never back down on a promise."

The watch fires, Shrunken Jim hisses, as though he's suddenly realized where we're headed. *We have to turn around! I'm cursed, remember?*

"Yeah, well," I say, remembering how the fires flared red last time I crossed over, and how I clearly hadn't imagined it after all, "you're not the only one."

19

Sure enough, the watch fires explode with a blood-red *boom* as we run into the darkness beyond. Embers leap upward to join the stars. Heat sears my cheeks. But we make it through. And we don't stop.

Lilou's flashlight beam trembles milky white ahead. My stomach does a little flip when I glance at her running beside me, face squashed in concentration as we navigate around the shadowed tussocks. Even when the dark makes Eelgrass Bog seem to crawl with maggot-breathed demons and long-dead monsters, it's impossible to feel afraid with Lilou.

Holloway's house has returned to its position above the tunnel entrance. The iron stilt-legs seem extra spidery in the nighttime, and the cheerful colors are swallowed up by shadows. But there's a light behind the stained-glass windows. Sure enough, when we barrel through the front door, Holloway is sitting in an armchair by the fireplace, a steaming mug of tea in her clawed fingers.

She heaves upright. "Pedrock? Starling? You came—"

"I know," I wheeze, "about the Endling Society."

Her face shutters, just like Oliver's when he noticed the

photographs. It closes up, and a lock slides into place. "I'm not sure I understand."

"That key let me into Oliver's library," I say. "I found a box like yours, and these photographs..." I trail off. Holloway isn't even looking at me properly anymore. Her eyes keep twitching to a far corner of the house where a couple of spun-reed hammocks are strung from the rafters.

One of the hammocks sags as though somebody is lying inside. "Is someone else here?" I ask, confused.

Holloway clears her throat. "No. Well. Yes. Your brother thought I gave you the library key on purpose, so he came to confront me about it. Except he's been fighting that curse of yours too hard. By the time he reached my house, he was almost unconscious on his feet." Misreading my horrified expression, she quickly adds, "Don't worry. He's just asleep."

"Oliver is here," I choke out. "Oliver is on Eelgrass Bog."

"It's the first time since ... well. The *incident*. But now he thinks I'm interfering." She paces distractedly. "I'm not interfering. It's been seventy years, so I didn't think he still kept Endling Society relics in the library! How was I supposed to know?"

To be fair, Shrunken Jim points out, *you could've just ... not given Kess the key.*

Holloway seems to notice Shrunken Jim for the first time. She looks guilty. "I didn't ... I didn't give it to her! She found it herself, and I ... There was no good excuse ..." The half witch stumbles over her words like uneven ground. "You're the one who can't do your job properly, Jimontheos! Each

159

time, you promise it's the last time. Yet here we are again!"

"Wait," I say. A horrid realization falls into place. "Jim, you know Holloway?"

His mouth-stitches sag. *Yes. I am sorry, Kess.*

If it wasn't for Lilou's arm around my shoulders, I think my knees would've crumpled and left me a muddly clump on the floor.

"That pickled head really can talk," Lilou says, dazed. "How come I can't hear him?"

"Because you aren't cursed," says Holloway wearily, "and Kess, well, is."

My throat closes. "Why?" I manage. "Why didn't anyone tell me?"

We have told you. Many times, Shrunken Jim explains. *But your memories rot away. That's your curse.*

"Usually it's easier than this." Holloway sighs. "Once or twice a decade, your curiosity gets too strong. You cross into Eelgrass Bog. I make you a cup of tea, then send you home. After a few weeks, you forget you were ever here. This is the first time you've mentioned the Endling Society. I suppose we have Miss Starling to thank for that." She wraps her arms tight around her middle, as though she's afraid of unraveling like an old knot. "Perhaps this mess is mostly my fault. I shouldn't have asked you to stay with me. I shouldn't have let you take the library key. And I should've tried harder to steer you away from the Endling Society. But it doesn't matter. These memories will fade in time too."

I let this sink in. "But what if I don't want them to fade?"

Holloway shrugs helplessly. "That's the problem with curses, Pedrock. They seldom care what we want."

It's why you have me, Shrunken Jim murmurs. *I made a bargain with Holloway after your curse was laid. She charmed this jar so I could exist outside of the Drowned World—it'd been so long since I'd seen the sky! Or pigeons! Or pickles!—and in exchange, I promised to keep you within the bounds of Wick's End as much as possible. I also promised to keep you company. The curse makes it difficult for people to remember you too. Plus regular humans grow up too fast, of course. Demons are much better friends.*

"I thought you came from my parents?" My voice is a squeak.

Once you forgot the truth, you believed whatever I told you.

"Right, well . . ." Lilou looks between me and Shrunken Jim with a puzzled expression. I realize she's only catching half of our conversation. "*I* want to know why Holloway didn't just explain all of this last time."

"Because remembering is messy," Holloway says. "I didn't want to tell Kess that her parents were dead. I didn't want her to be unhappy." She reaches out and squeezes both my hands, eyes dark and wide and glimmering like scraps of night sky. "We were friends once. And I hate that we can't go back to the Endling Society days. But it is best to let yourself forget, Pedrock."

Remembering is messy.

My mind spins back to the library: Oliver's scrawly notes, newspaper towers, and decades of diaries. All ways to pin down memories and stop them from flying away like birds. I guess he *did* manage to hold on to more memories than me. But I also think of how exhausted he always is, how he never has time to smile or joke or enjoy himself anymore, because he must've been battling the curse nonstop for seventy years. It's all very complicated. Because as much as I want to be angry at everyone for hiding the truth, as much as I feel like I'm tumbling off a mountainside . . . I get it. Everything *would* be easier if I'd been kept in the dark.

Some curses obviously don't want to be fought.

The thought is too big to process right now. I snatch my hands free from Holloway's grasp. My insides feel too full and too empty at the same time. I desperately want to grab Shrunken Jim's jar, just so I have *something* to hold on to, but he's watching me with the same uncertain expression as everyone else—like I might shatter at any second.

"We don't have to do this now," Holloway says softly. "I can make more tea, if you want. Or I can untie the other hammocks, and we can talk properly in the morning."

I want to argue that sleep is impossible after all the bombs dropped on me today. But I can hardly string two words together. I shrug and say, "Fine. Okay."

Holloway nods once and unties a row of hammocks. They're all woven from reeds and plant fibers and sway with the house's movements. One for Lilou. One for me. One for Holloway. And one for Oliver, already occupied.

I climb into the hammock farthest away from anyone else.

Pull a pillow over my ears. Try not to think of anything at all. It's easier said than done, of course. My head spins with ships and keys and curses, and I'm not sure which visions are dreams and which are memories.

Then, sometime in the small hours of the night, a crash startles me upright. It takes me a second to realize the sound is real–and coming from inside the house.

Oliver is awake.

20

I shrink into my hammock and pretend to stay asleep. But it's hard to keep my eyes closed. There's the shuffle of footsteps as Oliver stands up, then a mumbled curse as he must remember where he is. His breath comes quick and panicky. Something gets knocked sideways and breaks. He whimpers, "Ow!" alongside another string of very colorful curses. Shrunken Jim snorts a laugh from his perch on a rafter. Then there's silence, except for the shallow gasps of Oliver's breathing. I count to a hundred.

"Ollie?" I whisper.

No answer. I curse too and then roll out of the hammock. Holloway's hammock is empty. Lilou is here but unmoving, so I can't tell if she's woken up too. Oliver is curled up beside a shattered button jar, sucking at a gash on his thumb like a hurt kid on a playground.

"Let me see," I say.

Oliver flinches away from me, wide-eyed. "Kester? Why are *you* here?"

"I could ask you the same question," I point out.

"Where is Ivy?" He jumps upright and trips into a pile of

scrolls, sending them rolling across the floor. "She brought you here, didn't she? She must've. I can't believe that after all these years, she actually had the gall to interfere—"

"Stop," I say hotly. To my surprise, Oliver actually does. I grab his injured thumb, and he lets me. It's only a dribble of blood, barely more than a scratch.

Give him what for, Kess, Shrunken Jim whispers. Which is pretty bold of him, really, considering I'm furious at him too.

I open my mouth. Close it again. My heart seems to change its mind with every beat, dark to light, anger to softness. Thing is, I'm not sure how to handle this version of Oliver. He never looks scared like this.

"Kester," he begins.

"Kess," I correct.

"You shouldn't be here. If we're going to talk about what happened, we should do it back in Wick's End." Oliver glances nervously at the cat skeleton on the bookshelf. "I'm not sure what Ivy did, but I must've passed out—"

"You *did* pass out," I interrupt. "Then she brought you inside and took care of you."

Oliver snorts, sucking at his injured thumb.

"She also said you're exhausted because you've been fighting our curse too hard," I continue hurriedly so I don't lose my nerve. The word "curse" sticks on my tongue like a bad cockle. "I know you figured it'd be easier if you didn't tell me the truth. But easier isn't always better, right? I'm twelve years old, Ollie. If I'd understood, I could've helped fight too. I could've handled it."

I hope he doesn't hear how I'm trying to convince myself this is true.

A flash of pain crosses Oliver's face. His gaze flicks to the doorway. "That's the problem," he says, his old bitterness creeping back into view. "You *don't* handle it. Why do you think I lock the library? You've been *there* before too."

A chill slithers across my skin. "I—I have?"

"Once. About forty years ago." Oliver grimaces. "I lost three weeks of records trying to calm you down. Do you have any idea what that could've meant? Our memories only last about a month before they fade. I could've forgotten our curse altogether! I could've forgotten what I was trying to do, and what happened to us, all because you *couldn't handle it*."

Teeny-tiny memories wriggle through my brain cobwebs. Not images or moments, but feelings: panic and grief and helplessness. I didn't know about the Endling Society or the Drowned World then. I hadn't known what to do, and Oliver hadn't given me answers. So I guess I fell apart instead.

"Remembering is messy," I recite softly.

"Exactly. Which is why we have to go back to Wick's End so—"

"So I can forget again?" Anger shimmers through my voice. "You sound just like Holloway."

Oliver must not enjoy being compared to Holloway, because his lip curls and he spits out, "Here we go. Poor Kess, right? *I* spend every day keeping track of every minute that passes so I don't forget, while *you* sit around feeling sorry for yourself because you have to eat lunch alone."

"But—"

"*You* get to believe Mam and Da are still coming home. I *let* you keep that hope, Kester. I could've made you hurt with me, but I *didn't*." Oliver speaks quickly, like he's been desperate to say these things. "Words and pictures are memory triggers, see? If all you see are photographs from before the accident, that's all you'll remember. You'll forget the nasty stuff in between. You won't even realize how much time is passing if there's nothing to remind you. It's a thousand times easier than fighting every day, but no, *I'm* the bad brother, right?"

My whole body goes quiet. "The scratched-out dates on the display cases," I say. "That was you?"

Oliver nods.

I bite my tongue to stop an angry sob from escaping. I don't want to cry in front of Oliver and whoever else might be eavesdropping. But I bite too hard, filling my mouth with the taste of copper, and tears prick my eyes just the same.

"How come you got to make that choice?" I demand. "How come you didn't just forget like me from the start?"

He glares. "It doesn't matter."

"It *does*! It's my life too, Ollie!"

"See?" He groans. "Poor Kester. Always poor Kester. Nobody cares what I wanted! I've been alone this whole time, counting every second of the past seventy years. I lost everything too!"

"*I* cared!" I yell. "You haven't been alone! I've been here the whole time!"

I think of every sandwich I brought him. Every time I asked

for help with the Unnatural History Museum. Every unanswered knock at the library door. Every letter he promised to send to Antarctica. Fury grows inside my chest, tangled up with my grief worse than a bramble. Maybe the truth is painful and messy, but it's still the truth. And maybe it would've hurt less if we'd battled it together.

Oliver fiddles with the wire rims of his glasses. His fingers are shaking. "Doesn't matter now," he mutters. "I'll deal with Ivy later. You and I will go back to the Unnatural History Museum, and in a few weeks, we can return to normal."

"I can't just . . . forget again!" I say desperately. "Ollie, the museum is falling apart, and *you're* falling apart–"

"Oh, spare me," Oliver snaps. "What do you know? Face it, Kester, you can't even trust the right people."

"At least Holloway is nice to me."

In the dim light, Oliver looks more wax figure than boy. He smiles grimly, sallow skin stretching over his cheekbones. "Oh dear. Hasn't she told you?"

"Told me *what?*"

"Put the pieces together, Kester," he says. "Who do you think cursed us?"

21

It must be one shock too many, because suddenly, I can't feel a thing.

"She's only half witch," I say. "She doesn't even use magic."

"Yeah, because of what happened to us. And on top of being a very untalented witch, she's also spiteful, nasty, mean—"

"Go on," Holloway says. "Flatter me."

Oliver shrieks. He grabs a small letter opener and brandishes it at Holloway, who has appeared by the fireplace. Or maybe she's been here the whole time. It's hard to tell what she's thinking, but she seems disappointed, somehow.

"Put that down," she sighs. "You're embarrassing yourself, Pedrock."

"Yeah, well, it's true," Oliver says, but he doesn't sound very fierce. His voice cracks at the end. He gathers himself together and tries to jut his chin defiantly, though it looks more like a grimace. "You *did* curse us."

The air feels crackly with pressure, a whole book of unspoken stories passing between my brother and the half witch. I wonder if they've forgotten the rest of us exist. It feels like a private argument—except this is my life too.

"Undo it," I say.

Two heads snap around to face me.

"What?" Holloway says.

"You cursed us. So *un*curse us."

"She can't," Oliver scoffs. "Right, Ivy?"

Holloway glares, and I realize she's struggling to hold on to her calm right now. Then she pivots sharply to sit on the sofa. "Take a seat. Since nobody seems to be getting any sleep tonight, and we've already dredged up the Endling Society, we might as well tell Kess and Miss Starling the whole story."

Lilou's hammock creaks, and she rolls to her feet right away. She must've heard everything. But she doesn't look at me weirdly. Just fixes the buttons on her pajamas and plops onto the sofa, ready for whatever strangeness comes next. When she *does* look at me, it's with a reassuring, dimpled smile. The rest of us crowd around the sofas too. Even Shrunken Jim watches wide-eyed from the rafters. I pick at a tassel on a pillow and wait for someone to speak.

Holloway goes first. "I knew your parents," she tells me, "years ago, when they started collecting unnatural items from Eelgrass Bog. We didn't speak more than a handful of times, but they were . . . kind. I remember all the kind travelers. So I recognized their heart-glow in you, almost twenty years later, when you came to Eelgrass Bog after their deaths. Distant relatives were supposed to take care of you, I believe. But no one had come. It was just you, your brother, and his best friend, Jules Starling. You'd started a monster-hunting club together when you were younger children—you'd wanted to find unnatural creatures just like your parents—and you called yourselves the Endling Society. After your parents were lost, you used the society as a distraction."

"Grandpa was your best friend?" Lilou looks at Oliver.

He just scowls.

"We *all* became friends," Holloway continues. "I know secret things about Eelgrass Bog, so I was invited to join the Endling Society in exchange for my stories. It went both ways. You told me about ordinary life. I told you about the Drowned World. But that was my mistake. Because then you started to get ideas about *going* there."

"Rules work differently in the Drowned World," Oliver mumbles, kicking at the broken jar on the floor. "Unnatural magic can give people strange powers. Even powers over death itself."

"Oh," Lilou breathes, as if she suddenly understands.

I'm lost as ever. But with every word, flashes are cracking through my memory. Dancing barefoot in the rain. The smell of a wood-smoke bonfire. Holloway braiding feathers into my hair with clawed fingers. Jules playfully shoving Oliver into a puddle. Oliver mostly playfully shoving Jules into a bush. Swims in the river. Midnight bug catching. Hide-and-seek in birch thickets. And underneath it all, a heart-squeezing grief that just wouldn't disappear. My head begins to throb again.

"Those are bargains the Drowned World uses to trap you,"

Holloway says tightly, as though she's explained this many times before. "I made that mistake myself, long ago. If you'd succeeded—if you'd become witches—"

"It wouldn't have mattered, if we could've brought our parents back!" Oliver cries.

And there it is. *We could've brought our parents back.*

Faintly, faintly, I remember.

A hiss escapes Holloway's teeth. "That," she says, "is exactly what I believed when I was still human. I thought if I gained unnatural powers, I could bring my sisters back to life. But it—doesn't—work. It's a *trap*." She swallows. "I told you again and again, yet you wouldn't listen. Once the idea got into your heads, you were obsessed. You wanted to visit the Drowned World even if it swallowed you up for a thousand years and spat you out as witches."

"Maybe we didn't care," Oliver snaps.

"Maybe you should've cared," Holloway snaps back.

Kess? Shrunken Jim creases his eyebrow-stitches. *Are you okay?*

I nod, wiping my eye with my sleeve. This is a lot, but I know I have to hear the rest. This is my life they're talking about.

"One night," Holloway goes on, facing me, "you and your brother tried to sneak into the Drowned World. Jules noticed and went to stop you. But . . . the tunnel collapsed. You and Jules were badly injured. Oliver only escaped unharmed because he'd run farther ahead. And I realized if I didn't do something, you'd just keep trying until you got yourselves killed. Or worse." Holloway hiccups like she's on the edge of tears too. "I'd promised myself I'd never use magic again, because I didn't want to become more of a witch than I already was. But I had to protect you. You were only supposed to forget what I'd told you about the Drowned World, except..."

"Except you're the worst witch ever," Oliver mutters.

Grow up, Shrunken Jim retorts.

Oliver whips around to glare at Shrunken Jim. "Oh, sure, except I *can't* grow up. Because instead of forgetting about the Drowned World, the curse made *all* our memories rot away!"

"It almost worked," Holloway says a little defensively. "It was the hardest thing I'd ever done, and I thought I'd kept you safe from yourselves. Until ten years later, when Kess wandered back into the bog and she was still twelve years old."

"Exactly," Oliver says. "Worst witch ever."

I yank the pillow's tassel so hard it almost snaps. "I don't understand," I tell Holloway. "How can a curse go wrong?"

"Spells are crafted from special objects: locks of hair, favorite flowers, threads from clothes," Holloway explains. "Anything with value. Witches can add their own meanings to create charms or curses. But they won't activate unless they're brought to the Drowned World."

"The source of magic," I whisper, remembering Shrunken Jim's tales.

Shrunken Jim nods slowly. Green light from his jar spills across the rafters like we're somewhere sunken and strange too.

"But how did it go *wrong*?" I say. All this new information is making my head hurt, but I desperately want to understand. When I glance at Lilou, her brow is furrowed like she's trying her best to puzzle it all out too.

Holloway exhales. "I was angry after your carelessness hurt Jules. I thought I could keep my intentions pure, but the Drowned World saw the anger in my heart. It also saw that deep down, I . . . I wanted the Endling Society to go on forever.

"That's how charms become curses. Sometimes we want good things for bad reasons. Sometimes we want bad things for good reasons. Sometimes we want *all* of those things at the same time, and when our intentions get tangled, so does the magic." Holloway shrugs wearily. "The Drowned World saw that I wanted you to stay forever. It also felt my anger. It granted my wish and punished you at the same time, and that's why you haven't aged since. That's also why the curse cannot be broken. It's bound to the Drowned World—and it's still there, where I left it."

That's when she met me, Shrunken Jim says. *I saw her hide the curse and made my bargain.*

"Even if it's hidden," Lilou says determinedly, "we can find it and break it."

There's a long pause. Candles flicker. The house tilts and groans. Starlight filters through the painted glass windows.

"It's not that simple. The Drowned World doesn't like when magic is taken away or broken. There are creatures down there that could react to the disturbance. Creatures that are dangerous enough to cause damage to Eelgrass Bog *and* Wick's End." Holloway sounds defeated. "Plus, since you are both bound to the curse, breaking it might have . . . *effects*. Perhaps those seventy years might catch up all at once."

Cold spills down my spine. I imagine my bones powdering into dust. Silver bleeding through my hair.

"We could still try, right?" I say uncertainly.

Holloway touches one of the brambles in her hair. "Have you not listened? Don't you remember what happened to Dr. Stoat? The Drowned World is a hungry place. It will try to keep you forever—even if you escape, you might be a very different person." Her expression is haunted and faraway, as though she's imagining herself turned full monster a million miles underground. She hesitates, then lays a clawed hand on my knee. "Fighting it will only cause more trouble, Kess. You *have* to let yourself forget."

All eyes are on me. Even that stupid cat skeleton on the bookshelf. I try to absorb everything I've heard. My head rings with wispy memories of the Endling Society—with hurt and hope and secrets. But no matter how hard I try to string my thoughts together, I feel as empty and blown out as the basement hallways of the Unnatural History Museum.

Suddenly the house feels too small. There doesn't seem to be enough air left for all of us. I lurch upright, grab the nearest pair of rubber boots, and pull them over my socks.

"Where are you going?" Holloway blinks.

"Out," I say.

"It's the middle of the night."

I shrug.

"Kester—"

Let her go, Shrunken Jim says. *Just be careful, Kess.*

"I don't need your permission," I snap with more fierceness than I meant, but my feet carry me outside before I can apologize. Nobody tries to stop me.

22

As soon as I'm outside, I walk toward the edge of a lake-sized puddle. My rubber boots bite into the soggy ground. The stars reflected there wobble and break like banished ghosts. When I reach the edge, I grab a fistful of muck and lob it as hard as I can, and I yell and yell and yell so loud a couple of startled geese yell back. Air whooshes out of my lungs. I dig my fingers deep into the earth and make another mudball. I throw that one at the reflection of Holloway's spider-house, watching it splinter into shards.

I'm mad at Mam and Da. Why'd they need to take the Antarctica job? Why couldn't they have stayed in Wick's End? They didn't fix anything. They left us.

"Argh!"

I scoop up another gigantic mudball and throw it into the water. The *sploosh* spits water across my glasses, seeping into my clothes like cold, biting thorns. I think I'm crying, but it's too difficult to tell. I had no idea it was possible to feel so much at once.

I raise my arm to throw again, but my energy is slowly draining away. I close my fingers around the mud instead.

Mam once explained how peat is made from decomposing plants, a mixture of dead things and living things too tiny for our eyes to see. She was special like that, my mam. She made ordinary stuff seem magic. Maybe I've forgotten a whole lifetime, but I can still remember that.

The mud spills from my hand, gently raining around my feet. I lower myself down too. Damp seeps into my trousers. My reflection stares up at me from the black water, filthy and tired and lost.

"Mind if I join?"

I freeze. Then I jerk my head into a nod, keeping my eyes on the puddle as Lilou's reflection appears beside mine. She's wrapped herself in a pink woven blanket and has a second blanket draped over her arm.

She offers it to me. "Sorry. I know you probably want to be alone. But, um, I was worried you might get cold. I can leave again. Or not. It's up to you."

"'S okay," I mumble. After hesitating for a second, I accept the blanket and pull it over my shoulders. A tiny, poisonous part of me is mad at Lilou too. If she hadn't visited the Unnatural History Museum and shown me her grandpa's map, I never would've remembered stuff about the Endling Society. But that's unfair. Lilou never lied to me. I keep my mouth shut, just in case something horrible spills out that I don't mean.

"Should've brought my bow and arrows," Lilou says, crouching next to me. "It's only a plastic practice set from when I was obsessed with the fox version of *Robin Hood*, but it's more fun than chucking mud. Especially when you're angry."

I stay quiet.

"Once I shot an arrow at Simon. That was after I found out I'd grown allergic to peanuts." She chuckles softly. "Halloween was coming, and I wanted my Reese's Pieces. When you're six years old, that's like, a *huge* deal. I was also furious because my dads gave me foam arrows instead of real ones. But if they hadn't . . ." Lilou pauses. "Not sure why I'm telling you this. It isn't important."

I'm imagining a tiny Lilou furiously shooting arrows in her backyard and, despite everything, my lips twitch in the corners.

"Guess what I came out here to say is . . ." Lilou takes a deep breath. "No matter what you choose, Kess, I've got your back."

"Choose?" I echo, confused.

"Well, y'know. Whether or not to break your curse."

"You heard what Holloway said," I mutter. "It's stuck in the Drowned World. Breaking it would be impossible."

"'Impossible' is a very strong word. I used to think witches and magic were impossible until . . . well, a few hours ago." Lilou unfolds her grandpa's map from her pocket. "I've been thinking about what Grandpa's message really meant. He moved away from Wick's End when he was sixteen, so it would've been almost immediately after you got . . . y'know, cursed. He always said his parents dragged him to Canada because he got into too much trouble in Wick's End." She snorts. "I guess running away to Eelgrass Bog and coming back half-crushed by an underground tunnel is what he meant."

I squish my fingers into the ground. How nice for Jules Starling that he could just *leave*.

"I bet he felt guilty for abandoning you, even if it wasn't all his decision. He had all those unsent letters, right?" Lilou says, as if she can read my bitter thoughts. "He died pretty soon after we moved to Wick's End, but he must have seen you around town or something. He must've figured out that something went bad with Holloway's charm. And maybe that's why he chose to give me the map instead of anyone else—we're the same age, right? Maybe he thought I'd be the best person to reach out to you."

The idea is a shivery one. Did I meet Jules Starling as a dying old man, only to forget about it?

"Grandpa knew Holloway. Better than anyone, if those photos are anything to go by," Lilou continues with a small eye roll. "If he wrote *Break the curse*, that means he thought it was possible to . . . well, break the curse. He wouldn't have said that if he didn't believe it."

"Yeah, but what about the side effects Holloway mentioned?"

"Well, that's what I'm trying to say. I wanted to let you know, if you'd rather go back to Wick's End . . ." Lilou pauses. Her cheeks are pinker than the blanket. Then she blurts, "I won't forget you, Kess, even if you forget me."

With a *whumph* in my chest, I realize what she means.

If we try to reach the Drowned World, we could end up witches or worm meat or lost to nightmares like Dr. Stoat. But if we listen to Holloway and return to Wick's End without breaking the curse, my memories will keep rotting away until one day, I'll forget Lilou completely. And if Shrunken Jim is

180

right about the curse making it hard for people to remember *us*, maybe she won't have a choice either—maybe she'll forget me too. Even if she visits, even if I keep pictures and letters and memory triggers, she'll have to grow up. Meanwhile I'll stay the same. A broken dusty thing in an unnatural history museum that's quickly running out of time.

"I don't want to forget again," I say slowly. "I want to have a real life, not a cursed one."

"Are you sure?"

"Yes." My voice is quiet and small, but firm.

Could I actually reach the Drowned World and survive? Could I be brave enough, even if failure means losing everything I have left? Even if remembering means permanently accepting that Mam and Da are gone?

"It's not going to be easy, is it?" Lilou says, as though she can read my mind.

"No," I agree. "But . . . I think we have to try."

She nods. "So we have to figure out how to sneak into the tunnel without Holloway noticing—"

"Wait," I say. "Not *we*. Last time the tunnel made you sick after five minutes. Your grandpa almost died down there. You can't put yourself in that kind of danger."

"Sure I can."

"It's too risky."

Lilou sticks out her chin. "And what if I think you're worth the risk?"

I open my mouth to reply, but there's something about

her words that makes my breath spark in my throat. Like she's spoken something else underneath, something secret and daring.

My palms go sweaty. I find myself looking at Lilou, *really* looking at her. Freckles splashed across her nose. The silver glint of metal when she smiles. Black hair wound into a braid. Dazedly, I understand why Holloway used forbidden magic to try to keep us from being changed by the Drowned World. I wouldn't want Lilou to change for anything.

Truth is, nobody makes me feel seen like she does. She's a better friend than I could've dreamed of. But that tingly knot inside my chest makes me less and less certain that "friend" is a big enough word to cover everything that I feel. Lilou is my friend. But I also want to hold her hand, same as how Jules and Holloway held hands in that photograph. When a stray hair blows across her face, I want to brush it away. And when I look at her now, my heart double-jumps.

"Thing is . . ." I falter. "I . . . I like you. You're my best friend, but you're also . . . you're also . . ."

I grit my teeth. This was all so much easier in my head.

"Also?" Lilou whispers.

Words fall out like spilled marbles. "You can't come to the Drowned World because you're everything to me and I would rather drink a pail of liquefied toe fungus every day than see you get hurt."

My face burns. *Liquefied toe fungus?*

Except Lilou doesn't laugh. At first she just looks surprised.

Then she looks relieved, like she'd been waiting for *me* to laugh at her. "Good," she says finally, "because . . . um, you're kind of everything to me too."

My heart pounds. "Really?"

She nods. "Y'know how . . . how there are people you like, and then people you *like*-like?"

I think again of Jules and Holloway holding hands. Of holding Lilou's hand. Of how her dads always found a way to gently brush each other as they moved through their kitchen, and of the special smiles Mam and Da shared in their photographs. It turns my whole body into melted ice cream.

"Yeah," I say. "I—I think I get what you mean."

"Do you actually?" Lilou's eyes are wide and shining with starlight. "It's just, I remember in fifth grade when I asked Marcia Ratton to a school dance, she said we couldn't like-like other girls, only boys, and I guess I'm always scared that . . ." She shakes her head in frustration. "I never know how to talk about this stuff."

She isn't the only one. I don't even know how to *think* about this stuff. I've spent so much time worrying about the Unnatural History Museum, I've never let myself wonder about the future, or growing up, or crushes or dances or girls or boys.

"Well"—I clear my throat—"for what it's worth, I would've gone with you to the dance."

Lilou brightens right up. "There's another one at the end of sixth grade. Maybe you could come as my . . . well, as my date?"

"Date?" I choke out.

"Yeah. If you want." She tries to say it casually, but I can tell she's using all her courage right now.

"C-course," I stammer. "That would be really, really good."

Wind shivers across the water. Our thumbs brush together. My breath is almost stopped, but inside, my heart is exploding into happy fireworks.

Even if the Drowned World changes everything, trying to break the curse will be worth the risk so I won't ever forget moments like this. The future suddenly feels enormous.

I just have to find a way to get there.

I point toward Holloway's house. "How can we unblock the tunnel?"

Lilou considers. Her hand is still touching mine. "Depends. If I stayed behind, I suppose I could figure out a distraction."

"Perfect," I say, relieved.

"But you shouldn't go alone. Maybe you could take Oliver with you. Or your demon-in-a-jar."

Just thinking about them and their secrets makes my temples throb. I wrinkle my nose and say, "Or not."

Lilou quirks an eyebrow. "Isn't your demon *from* the Drowned World?"

I'm about to point out how he's also a rotten-skulled liar when I remember something he said earlier: *I saw her hide the curse and made my bargain.*

Shrunken Jim knows what the curse looks like. More than that, he knows where it was hidden.

"All right," I say reluctantly. "Jim can come."

Lilou nods. "Good. You better survive in one piece, Kess Pedrock. Otherwise you're in big trouble."

"I promise. At *least* one piece."

She swats at me and I dodge, laughing.

"So what's your distraction plan?" I ask.

Lilou flashes her special silvery smile. "Leave it to me."

23

My teacup is shaped like an upside-down mushroom. There are even black frills around the edge, tickling my lip whenever I pretend to sip. *Pretend* because I'm not certain the purplish liquid inside is actually tea. It smells of raindrops and blueberries and old wood, which isn't exactly unpleasant—but I'm pretty sure even blueberry tea isn't supposed to sparkle.

The mood inside the house is very, very awkward. Oliver is sulking by a bookshelf, pretending to read the volumes perched there so he doesn't have to acknowledge us. Holloway's spine is knife straight as she sits on the sofa, knuckles tight around the handle of her teacup. I reckon they were both arguing while we were gone. Shrunken Jim watches from the rafters with creased eyebrow-stitches. Lilou is on a stool closest to the fireplace, still wrapped in the bright pink blanket. It was her idea to make tea. She helped Holloway fetch the cups and gather leaves from all the proper jars—FOR SERENITY and FOR CALM, mostly—but same as me, she hasn't taken a single sip.

"This is nice," Holloway says.

From the bookshelf, Oliver scoffs.

"We don't have to fight." She tries to smile, though it comes out tense and anxious. "We can enjoy each other's company, just like old times, then carry on with our lives—"

"We can't," I say quietly. "You have to let us try to break the curse."

Holloway's smile strains. "I thought I explained why that was impossible."

"Maybe it isn't. Maybe we'll come back fine," I argue. "Maybe it'll break easily, and the creatures will stay asleep—"

"I said no," Holloway snarls. Then she exhales through her sharp teeth and takes a long gulp of tea. Calmer, she says, "We all make mistakes. You shouldn't have ignored me and snuck into the tunnels seventy years ago. I shouldn't have interfered with your memories. But you were my only friends, and I was . . . I *am* looking out for you. I kept you from making a very dangerous decision, and I won't let you make it again now."

"How noble," Oliver mutters.

"But things are different now. I don't *want* to become a witch; I don't *want* magic," I point out, folding my arms. "Breaking a curse isn't the same as trying to raise the dead."

Holloway glares. "It doesn't matter what you are *trying* to do. I never *tried* to wipe away all your memories. I never *wanted* to live forever. But the Drowned World doesn't care, and it will ruin you just the same!"

There's so much hurt behind Holloway's words. I imagine how it must feel to live hundreds of years alone. Perhaps that's why she cared about saving us so much—because it was too late to save herself from the Drowned World's magic. Still, I'm convinced that I have something Holloway didn't.

Reasons to come back.

I try a different approach. "Thing is," I begin, "the Unnatural History Museum is running down. It won't last another seventy years without visitors. If we forget how much time is passing, we won't be able to fix it."

"That's why my work is important," Oliver says tersely.

I shoot him a glare. "I told you, I could've helped—"

"Says the kid who kept interrupting my work every five minutes!"

"Kess mentioned wanting new bones to bring visitors back," Holloway interrupts loudly. "I suppose if you both promised to stop fighting the curse—and to stay away from the Drowned World—I might be able to solve your problem."

She sets down her empty teacup and drags out a heavy wooden chest, carved with unicorns and castles and wild-petaled flowers with ugly human faces. It's big enough to fit a person inside. Bigger, even. She flips open a clasp, then unrolls a layer of green velvet to reveal something golden underneath.

At first I think it's a sculpture. I've seen oddly colored bones before, of course, but never *gold*. And I've never seen a deer skull as large as this.

It's spectacular. The eye sockets are dark and fathomless like they're holding entire universes inside. A single branching antler sprouts from the left temple. In the box, carefully laid against the velvet, I can see vertebrae and ribs, femurs and a pelvis, a mandible and scapula. Each is glimmering gold and at least five times the size of regular deer bones. Even Oliver stares in wonder.

"Wow," I breathe, forgetting to be troubled for a moment. "What is this from?"

"*Aurum venatione cervorum*," Holloway says with a note of pride. "The golden stag of Eelgrass Bog. Perhaps the rarest species of megafauna to live in the past ten thousand years, never before cataloged by a human scientist. I found it buried beneath a long-gone riverbed after I first escaped the Drowned World. It inspired the symbol of the Endling Society."

"It did?" Oliver splutters. "You told us the golden stag was imaginary! Why didn't you show us then?"

She pauses. "Because I was worried you might take it and run. This is the only complete skeleton in existence."

Without really thinking, I've reached for the skull. The golden bone is cold and mirror smooth. It's exactly what I wanted—an unnatural artifact from the Endling Society. People would come from beyond Wick's End to see this. I'd have my very own plaque: CATALOGED BY KESS PEDROCK. We would have enough money to restore the Unnatural History Museum to how it was before, before Mam and Da left, before the exhibits began to decay. Back to when everything was simple and perfect and right.

Except . . . it wouldn't be the same. Not really. Mam and Da would still be gone. I'd still be full of holes and cobwebs. Slowly, surely, Lilou and I would forget each other. Even if we went to the dance together, my memories would rot away, and we'd never have any future to look forward to.

"Kess?" Oliver watches me warily. I can't tell what he thinks about the offer; whether he would agree to stop fighting the curse and leave his notes and diaries behind. But it doesn't matter. For once, I know exactly what *I* think.

I'm not going to lock my secrets into a box and pretend the past never happened. After all, there are much more precious things than buildings. Whatever happens to the Unnatural History Museum, I still want to be myself—because *myself* is enough.

Which is why I'm going to break the curse.

My eyes catch Lilou's. While we've been focused on the deer skull, she has quietly snuck over to the fireplace. One of her hands is clenched around a stilt-steering lever. A silent question hovers between us.

I nod.

Then the house lurches sideways, *very* sharply. The chest slides across the floor and crashes into a bag of soda cans. Flowers tumble from the rafters. Shrunken Jim shrieks as his jar sloshes. Oliver grabs the edge of a table but trips over anyway. Holloway is thrown onto the sofa. My shoulder smacks into the wall.

"Sorry," Lilou says innocently. "Pulled that lever a bit too hard."

"Starling," Holloway hisses. "What are you doing?"

"Well, I *tried* to give you sleepy tea, but I must've miscalculated, because you aren't very asleep. I've never been much good at cooking. Unless it's snickerdoodles." Lilou shrugs. "So I'm improvising."

"Don't touch—"

But Holloway doesn't finish her sentence. Lilou yanks another lever, and the house hurtles in a different direction, sending everyone tumbling to the floor. My teacup spills. Shrunken Jim's jar tips, and automatically, I catch him before he hits the floor.

Thanks, Kess! he gasps.

"Starling, stop this! You're going to—" Holloway cuts off as the house lurches and a ball of elastic bands narrowly misses her head. "You're going to break it!"

"It's a bit like a video game controller," Lilou muses. "I'll get the hang of it in a second. Hold tight!"

There's an earsplitting *thunk*, then the unmistakable sensation of the house moving. Not just tilting. The stilt-legs groan and start to walk away, which must mean the tunnel entrance below is now uncovered. Holloway tries desperately to reach the fireplace, but she can't seem to take a step without slipping over. Her movements are clumsy, and I guess Lilou's sleepy tea worked a little after all—plus the house is sloped at a sharp angle, with Lilou at one end and the rest of us tumbled into the other.

Lilou looks at me, eyes bright with mischief and something else, something fragile. Like she's scared and trying very hard not to be. "It's your call, Kess," she says. "What do you want?"

I know there's only one way to go from here. We've been reaching backward for too long already. It's time to go forward.

"I'm going to the Drowned World," I say resolutely. "I'm going to fix this."

"Kess Pedrock, don't you dare!" Holloway shouts. "Starling, for worm's sake!"

Oliver gapes at me, then Lilou, realization dawning. "Wait—"

But I'm done with waiting. I clutch Shrunken Jim's jar close to my chest and haul myself upright using a toppled cabinet. I'm itching to say something heartfelt to Lilou, in case I end up lost in the Drowned World.

Then Lilou's hand slips, and the house lurches violently in the other direction. Holloway reaches toward me. She's stumbling properly now, blinking too fast. I dodge free and crawl to the door and turn the handle. Any brilliant last words I might've said are cut off by a yell as I fall out of the house and land—*splat*—five feet below in the muck.

Dazed, I blink up at the house, twisted into a weird sideways angle above me. Lilou must have gotten control of the levers again, because a heartbeat later, it straightens itself and begins to run crookedly in the direction of Wick's End. I'm left alone.

And finally, I can see the tunnel entrance to the Drowned World.

24

I t's quiet underground. Not entirely silent, thanks to the dripping roots above my head. But it's the kind of quiet that makes me feel very small and alone. The tunnel stretches darkly. Even with the greenish glow from Shrunken Jim's jar, I can't see more than a few meters ahead. I take a steadying breath, but my pulse races like a rabbit. Oh, vermin, it's dark down here.

Kess? Shrunken Jim says.

"Yeah?"

I'm sorry I lied to you. About your parents. And . . . well, everything.

I push up my glasses with a shaky finger. "Why'd you tell me those Drowned World stories, if you wanted me to stay away?"

Shrunken Jim pauses for a long time. *Because sometimes I wanted to tell you the truth. And sometimes I didn't. You never stopped being curious, and I—I never completely stopped missing the place I came from.*

"Were you ever my friend?" My voice catches. "Or were you just pretending because Holloway told you to?"

Kester Wynn Pedrock, he says firmly, *you are the most stupendous acquaintance a shriveled-up demon-in-a-jar could possibly possess. Even without a heart, I care for you very much.*

"You were as bad as Oliver."

We were both doing what we thought was right, but doing it the wrong way. Maybe that's why we always disliked each other. Shrunken Jim sighs. *I swear on all the pickles in the world, I will not lie to you again.*

"Even about the nasty stuff?" I say.

Especially about the nasty stuff.

"Jim?"

Yes?

"Is your full name really Jimontheos?"

A laugh escapes from his mouth-stitches. Then I'm laughing too, despite the gloom and the fear in my bones, and I think maybe this is what it feels like to forgive someone.

Indeed, I am Jimontheos. Shrunken Jim laughs again. *Demon formidable and extraordinaire. I'm quite impressive outside of my jar, actually, but this form is necessary for living topside in Wick's End. And let me tell you, I'd consider stuffing myself into an even smaller jar if it meant I got to be your friend for another seventy years.*

"Don't push it," I say. But I'm smiling too.

We continue deeper into the tunnel, one boot in front of the other. I tell myself that's all I have to do—nothing heroic or wild, just one boot in front of the other without turning back. But my heart continues to pound. The shadows seem heavy enough to touch.

"Jim?"

Yes, Kess?

"Do you think I'll be able to break the curse?"

If anyone can visit the Drowned World and escape unscathed, it's you, Shrunken Jim says carefully. *I'll help wherever I can.*

I nod. It'll have to be enough.

As we go deeper and deeper, the air thickens with that awful rotten-egg peat smell. It tingles up my nostrils and makes my whole body feel as though it's being bathed in chemicals, the embalming kind Mam and Da used to preserve specimens. I pick up my pace. This time I'm paying closer attention, so I notice when the mud walls start to glimmer with world-serpent scales. It's hard to believe it was only a couple of days ago that I was here with Lilou, figuring all I'd find on Eelgrass Bog was a handful of bones. I hurry past the scales without stopping to admire them, even as they glint prettily in the jar-light.

One boot in front of the other.

Suddenly the tunnel plunges downward, steep enough that I almost fall forward. My stomach churns. I have to squint to make sure the ground doesn't drop off into a bottomless chasm.

"They should've built handrails," I mutter shakily.

Agreed. Make sure to tell the world-serpents when you see them, Shrunken Jim says. *No handrails! Those monsters!*

I roll my eyes and start to navigate the slope. It's easier said than done. The rotten-egg smell is turning my stomach inside out. Even though I'm not usually bothered by dark spaces, as dirt keeps raining down on my head, I'm uneasy about how deep we've traveled. Was this how the accident happened, when Jules Starling tried to follow us into the Drowned World? Was he scared? Were *we* scared? I try to imagine me and Oliver running together into the dark, hoping to change ourselves into the kind of witches that could conjure the dead. It only makes my head hurt.

A sprinkle of dirt plops onto Shrunken Jim's jar. He flinches. *Something isn't right*, he murmurs.

I glance warily upward. Either the eggy air has messed with my senses, or the walls are trembling, like there's an earthquake happening nearby. More dirt falls onto my upturned face. My rabbit heart races, and my palms are sticky around Shrunken Jim's jar.

"One boot in front of the other," I say to myself, aloud this time. Which is exactly what I do. Deeper, darker, onward, faster, even as the tingly not-right feeling gets stronger and stronger.

I hurry until I'm almost running. Down, down, down. My breath comes quick and shallow. The rumbling gets louder, and the deeper I go, the more dirt falls from the ceiling until it feels like I'm caught in an underground rainstorm. Panic claws up my throat.

Ke-ess, perha-aps this is a sign we sho-ould turn arou-ou-ound, Shrunken Jim yells, bouncing around in his jar as I run. *Magic can b-beget magical rea-ac-actions, so it'll get more da-angerous the dee-eeper you go! Like the wa-atch fires, remember?*

"We're fine!" I yell back. But a thick chunk of peat breaks loose and knocks my head sideways as if to say, *Challenge accepted, little girl.* I remember what Mam told me about peat mud, about how it can be a thousand years old only one meter deep. The stuff falling on me now must be ancient.

Older than people, maybe. I blink away dizzy stars and keep running. I try to ignore the crumbling tunnel and the murky, panicky part of me that remembers being in this situation before. Instead, I think of rooftop picnics, grilled cheese sandwiches, and the way Lilou said "date" like it was the most hopeful word in the universe. Memories we can still make. Adventures we haven't had yet. Stories waiting to be told.

I think of the future.

Kess, Shrunken Jim says urgently. *Holloway isn't here to dig you out this time, and I really–*

But he doesn't finish his sentence. Because that's when the tunnel caves in.

There's an earsplitting groan, then a waterfall of muck pours over me. I shriek and throw up my arms. Not that it does any good.

Run! Shrunken Jim yells.

I try. But my mouth and eyes and ears are full of dirt. I bump into something hard, desperately trying to keep ahold of Shrunken Jim's jar. More dirt pours down. My knees smack into the ground. I attempt to get up, but I can't see—everything is shaking–

Kess! Shrunken Jim's light vanishes from my hand.

I can't even scream. A rock falls and pins down my coat. Another one crunches into my ankle, sending needles of pain sparking through my whole leg. My glasses are cracked. The bitter taste of dirt is thick in my mouth, and all I can think is *not again, not again, not again.*

"Kester! C'mon, you have to run!"

I try to tell Shrunken Jim that I'm stuck. But I just get another lungful of dirt. Dimly, through the roar of the tunnel collapsing, I hear him swear. Shrunken Jim never swears like that.

Hands grab under my armpits and haul me to my feet. I yelp when I have to put weight on my ankle, but the hands don't let go. For a hopeful second, I think Lilou has come to my rescue.

Except Lilou doesn't have pointy-thin arms and the mildewy stench of a composted tea bag.

I spit out a wad of dirt. "Oliver?"

"No, it's the tooth fairy," he snaps. "Is anything broken? Can you stand?"

I nod numbly. "How—"

"Here's your ridiculous gnome," he interrupts, shoving Shrunken Jim's jar into my arms. The light has dimmed and the glass is cracked, but Shrunken Jim is giving Oliver a poisonous death glare, so he must be all right.

There's no time for explanations now. We have to crouch to fit into the remains of the tunnel, and after I shake some muck from my ears, I hear a noise that sounds horribly like rushing water. And it's getting louder very, very quickly.

Oliver and I share a wide-eyed glance.

"Oh, vermin," he says.

I reach a hand into the dark. "Maybe there's– Oh! Look! Here!"

Around knee height, the crumbling wall has opened up to

reveal a second tunnel, barely wider than a rabbit hole. I have to get down on my knees again to peer through, but *this* tunnel isn't raining dirt. Which means it's the only option we have left.

"Nope," Oliver says. "No way. We can't go *deeper*."

"Surprise," I say grimly. "Turns out we can."

I grab his bony wrist and yank him through the hole, just as the rest of the big tunnel collapses.

25

We're sealed inside like a tomb. Aside from the dying jar-light, it's pitch-black, and I can't raise my head more than a few inches before it hits the ceiling. The air feels very thin. Cold sweat gleams across my skin, and my shirt clings to my back.

"I hate Eelgrass Bog," Oliver mutters.

Poor Pedrock, Shrunken Jim says. *We should have thought about that before we asked you to come. Except . . . wait . . . I don't remember inviting you anywhere?*

"You talk a lot for a tongueless goblin," Oliver snaps.

Goblin? Who are you calling goblin?

I suck in a shallow breath and try not to panic about how we're going to reach the surface again. Slowly, slowly, I crawl forward. My ankle throbs, rocks scrape my knees, and damp seeps farther into my clothes. But after a few painful minutes, the tunnel yawns wide enough for me to stand. Thank *goodness.* I raise Shrunken Jim's jar . . . and my jaw drops.

"What have you stopped for?" Oliver grumbles, shuffling behind me. Then I hear him gasp in shock.

The space ahead grows longer and wider before our eyes, stretching like some kind of foldaway telescope until it's twice the size of the previous tunnel. And that isn't the weirdest part. Instead of mud or roots or even serpent scales, the walls are coated with something spongy that could be moss—except for the fact that it's glowing a bright, rose-petal pink.

"Are you seeing this?" I ask.

Oliver nods, dazed. I can see him properly now, filthy shirt and filthy trousers and filthy hair and filthy face. He looks like a dug-up corpse. Probably I do too. But despite the mess and the fear, a warm bubbly feeling grows inside my chest. Before he can open his mouth, I've thrown my arms around his shoulders.

"Um," he says.

I squeeze him tighter. "You came after me."

He pats me awkwardly on the back. "Yeah, well. I can't expect you to break this curse alone."

"Is Lilou okay? Who's controlling the house?"

Oliver winces. "Ivy's pretty groggy from that tea, but your friend isn't very good at steering. I almost broke my knees jumping out. Last I saw, they were headed toward the watch fires." He must notice my worry, because he adds, "Your friend is a Starling. If she's anything like her grandfather, she'll be fine."

I step away from the hug, hoping he's right.

Oliver turns to face the pink stuff on the walls. Maybe it's the glow, but he looks almost embarrassed. "I just, um, want to say that I never meant for things to turn out so . . . messy," he mumbles. "With your memories, I mean. And everything else. I honestly thought it would be better for you to forget."

My spine stiffens. "It wasn't your decision."

"No," he says quietly. "It wasn't."

"Are you ever going to tell me what happened? The day we got cursed, I mean?"

He hesitates for a long time. The pink walls glitter like galaxies. Then he says, "It's foggy, even for me. All I remember is that when the tunnel collapsed, I was farther ahead, so I escaped unhurt. Jules caught the worst of it, but you . . . It still took you several days to recover."

My body trembles as though it can still remember. *Dark, no air, broken bones.*

"The second Ivy planted the curse, I felt it," Oliver continues. He's still looking at the wall instead of me. "It was as if someone had suddenly stuffed my skull with cobwebs. I confronted her, but she wouldn't tell me the details of what she'd done—I think she was still messed up from returning to the Drowned World. So I ran back to Wick's End with you. Jules left with his parents. And although it took me a while to realize our memories were disappearing, I figured it out eventually."

"Then you started keeping notes," I finish. "And you never told me about the curse."

Oliver sniffs, wiping his nose on his sleeve. "I didn't know how."

A lump grows in my throat. I can't say *it's okay*, because it isn't. But I'm not sure this is the right time or place to get into it; I'm not sure I'm ready. So instead I mutter, "Just promise you won't shut me out again. No more locked doors, okay?"

He almost, almost smiles. "Sure. No more locked doors." He

slumps tiredly against a wall—then jumps backward in alarm. Darkness blooms from where he touched the moss, like he's spilled ink from his fingertips. It spreads and creeps and grows.

"Careful!" I cry.

I don't want the whole tunnel to go dark again. My heart is still hammering from how close we came to getting buried alive—again. But when I look nearer, I see something growing out of the darkness, unfurling like a flower's petals. *Mold spores.* I recognize them from the Unnatural History Museum. Except these spores aren't awful and icky and growing between cracks in bathroom tiles. They're as delicate as dandelion puffs and glow a deep, shimmery green. When I touch the pink stuff, more spores bruise beneath my fingers.

"Wild," I breathe. And I smack my whole hand into the tunnel wall, watching the imprint of my fingers grow bigger and bigger.

Very clever, Shrunken Jim says dryly. *When the rest of the tunnel collapses, I can't wait to spend eternity watching you finger-paint.*

"Is he always this miserable?" Oliver asks.

I swipe my hand in a zigzag across the wall. "Almost as miserable as you."

Of course, Shrunken Jim isn't wrong. We're in too deep to get distracted. Trailing my fingertips, I raise his jar and walk down the tunnel, hoping it doesn't stretch onward forever. Oliver falls into step beside me. The tunnel widens until it's practically a cavern. Pink moss glimmers overhead like fireflies, swirling with dark green from our touch. My heart beats against my rib cage as we go deeper. There's a thrill plucking at my insides, scared but excited.

We're getting closer to the Drowned World. I can feel it.

The cavern narrows again. Holes start to pepper the walls, as though dozens of other offshoot tunnels have started to converge. For a moment, I'm worried we've walked straight into a maze—until I notice an archway cut through the dirt, right where most of the smaller tunnels end. Words in a strange language are scrawled around the threshold, and someone has etched a tiny serpent beside it all. It seems achingly old.

"Oh my gosh," Oliver murmurs. "It's . . . a staircase?"

I bring Shrunken Jim's jar closer, hardly believing my eyes. Oliver's right. A real, actual staircase spirals downward on the other side of the archway. Each step is yellow white and dipped in the middle from wear. It's hard to see with my glasses all cracked, but there's something about the pocked surface of the stairs that reminds me of—

"Bone," I gasp. "It's a *bone staircase*."

Oliver curses for real. "What kind of skeleton is this big?"

World-serpent, Shrunken Jim says in awe. *This must've been a spine, once upon a time.*

A laugh escapes me. I should be freaked out, but instead, the thrill inside me swells. This place is wondrous. I run down the bone staircase, hesitation melting away. Oliver follows close behind. Our arms stay outstretched, and wherever we touch, twinkling green spores dance across the darkness. It reminds me of a blooming garden. A beautiful, underground bone garden.

"We're really going to the Drowned World!" I pant excitedly. I know getting there is only a small part of the battle—getting out will be harder—but I can't help my excitement. I've heard Drowned World stories for years. Now I'm actually going to see it.

Through the gloom, golden light sparks up ahead. We must be miles deep now. Deep enough that the peat has turned to rock, still glimmering with moss and mold. I wouldn't be surprised if that new light is coming from the burning center of the earth. The air fizzes with something old and powerful and strange, and I feel it right down in the secret places of my heart.

Magic. It has to be magic.

"You can show us where Holloway hid the curse, right?" I ask Shrunken Jim. "You know what we're looking for?"

Of course, he says importantly. *We'll find it, no problem; the curse is made from parts of you. You're connected, so you should be able to feel it as we get close to it.*

I know Shrunken Jim is telling the truth. I can already feel a tug, like my bones know that a part of me is hidden somewhere close.

The important thing is not to become distracted by the cursed creatures, Shrunken Jim continues. *No matter what you're offered, no matter what you see or hear, do not enter into any bargains. Oh, and try not to wake the megafauna, lest you doom humanity to an apocalypse of earthquakes.*

"An apocalypse of earthquakes?" Oliver pales.

Shrunken Jim bobs his head in a shrug. *It will be fine, as long as you listen to my instructions.*

"Great," Oliver says sourly. "Should've known it would all come down to Kess's pet ghoul."

We trip down the last few bone steps. I throw out my arms to make sure I don't stumble into a wall. Or a monster. But no sooner have we rounded the next corkscrew than I have to clench my eyes shut because of the brightness.

We've reached the Drowned World.

26

At first I can't see anything through the brightness. Just gold and gold and gold. There are also sounds: the *shush-shush* of water somewhere close by, echoing around a space that feels as gigantic as a cathedral. A humming, too, snatches of a song that tickle goose bumps across my skin.

When my eyes finally adjust, I have to bite down a scream.

We're surrounded by creatures.

They hide behind pillars of gleaming rock that stretch up, up, up into a ceiling that's covered by swirling pink light. They hover by the shores of a golden river that seems bigger than an ocean. They have bog weed for hair and flowers blooming through their skin, antlers branching from their temples, over-sized ears curved like woodland animals'. Ink-black eyeballs and needle-thin teeth that drip to their chins. They wear rags and fur and, sometimes, nothing at all. One walks on slender hooves instead of feet. One has mushrooms growing from their spine. And all of them—dozens and dozens—are looking at us.

Oliver gives a strangled whimper.

"What are they?" I manage to say. Chills race from my head to my toes.

Witches, all of them, Shrunken Jim says grimly. *This is what happens if you stay in the Drowned World for too long. Remember what I said about getting distracted.*

So this is what Holloway was scared of becoming, scared for us to become. Horror and awe make my blood run cold. These witches make the fossils in the Unnatural History Museum seem no better than the soda cans Holloway keeps in her house. Here in the Drowned World, *unnatural* isn't just a whisper or a rumor or a ghost story. It's real. It's alive.

And it's everywhere.

Shrunken Jim yells again for us to move, but I'm frozen numb. The cavern stretches farther than my eyes can see. The light is gold and pink, flickering like there are candles buried deep within the rock. There are objects down here too. Giant lost things swallowed by the bog. Torn-sailed boats bob on the golden river. Crunched-up cars are draped with moss in damp, dark corners. And then there are bones, piled around the witches' feet and stuffed into holes that riddle the rock like honeycomb. Skulls. Ribs. Femurs. Animal. Human. And megafauna, three times the size of the rest. Some are neatly stacked in burial piles. Some are tangled up with twine and ribbon and shocks of hair so old, they've turned the color of dust. Those are the charms, I reckon. I can feel the magic pouring off them, thick and buzzing like mayflies in summer.

Somewhere in the rocks one of those charms—one of those *curses*—belongs to us. We just have to wade through a whole sea of witches to find it. Dread makes me shudder. After this, I'm never going to be afraid of the bog mummies at night again.

Move slowly, Shrunken Jim instructs. *No eye contact. No sudden movements. Just follow that pathway to your left.*

It takes an awful lot of concentration to do as he says. My feet suddenly feel very heavy. One foot. Another foot. Dozens of twinkling eyes follow my every movement. I don't realize I'm holding my breath until I stumble, and a *whoosh* of air escapes my lungs.

Careful, Shrunken Jim says.

"Sorry," I whisper.

None of the witches have moved. And neither has Oliver. When I search for him, he's still frozen on the bottom of the bone staircase, mouth open, grubby face washed with flickering gold. Quickly, I double back and loop his arm through mine. He doesn't pull away.

"C'mon, Ollie," I say. "You made it this far."

"I'm not sure I'm awake anymore," he says, dazed.

"You are. See?" I squeeze his arm. "And I'm here too."

He inhales. "Okay."

Shrunken Jim just rolls his eyes. We walk at a snail's pace because the ground is so uneven. My hip bumps against stalagmites, and we have to keep ducking under rocky arches. Charms glimmer like fallen wishing-stars. A long time ago, there must've been lots more people who decided to try their luck with the Drowned World's magic. I wonder what they were placed here for. How many worked, and how many became curses? How many were brought down here by desperate people who never returned to the surface again?

It isn't so bad, a voice says.

I jump, almost losing my grip on Shrunken Jim's jar. A witch has appeared from behind a rock pillar, close enough that I can smell the moss-and-rot stench clinging to its fur-covered body. Live insects weave through its ankle-length hair.

You are missing something, the witch says softly, circling us. A centipede curls around its throat. *I can feel the holes in your hearts. Don't worry. This is the place of bargains and dreams. If you stay with us, we can teach you magic.*

Back off, Shrunken Jim snarls. *Keep walking, Kess.*

I'm more than happy to listen to him. I chew the inside of my cheek to stop myself from gagging on the witch stench, and we go on. Around stalagmites and something that looks like a rhinoceros skull, except it's double the size. But before I can concentrate on finding our curse, another witch materializes beside us. I jump and almost bite off my tongue in alarm.

A different bargain, perhaps, it purrs. *How would you like the strength of ten?*

A silver-skinned witch joins in. *Stay, and we will show you how to conjure fire.*

We will show you how to craft curses and charms of your own.

We will show you how to turn pebbles into diamonds.

We will show you how to speak with the dead.

Oliver stops.

I pivot back to face him. "Ollie. C'mon."

"But what if it is possible?" His expression has gone faraway, bursting with hurt and hope. "What if we were right seventy years ago? Maybe there *is* magic that can let us see Mam and Da again."

There is, there is, the witch chants. It reaches out a hand with seven webbed fingers. *Stay here, and I can show you how.*

"No," I say, "we can't! Remember what Holloway said? The longer we stay down here, the harder it'll be to leave!"

"So? We've lost so much time already," Oliver says. "What's a little more, if we get to speak with Mam and Da?"

The magic in the air grows stickier. My head spins. Even though I'm scared, even though I can feel the tug of our curse somewhere nearby, even though I know we're flies wandering through a spider's web, a spark of yearning is growing in my chest too.

Don't be stupid, Shrunken Jim growls. *Walk away, both of you.*

"But this is Mam and Da." Oliver's voice breaks. "We . . . I need them back."

I shut my eyes and imagine Mam tucking me in at night, Da's booming laughter, the four of us just . . . being a family together.

My fingers twitch toward the witch's outstretched hand.

But Holloway and Shrunken Jim have warned us time and time again that magic is dangerous. The Drowned World didn't give Holloway her sisters back. My parents could come back *wrong*, if they came back at all. And we could be stuck down here forever, while the real world spins onward without us.

The Drowned World devours people with promises, not teeth.

"Ollie," I begin, opening my eyes, "I don't think—"

But it's too late. The space in front of me is empty, just chunks of gold-washed rock and the thrum of nearby curses.

Oliver is gone.

And so is the witch.

27

"No!" I cry. "No, no, no! Where'd he go?"

The witch could probably tell you were about to refuse, Shrunken Jim says grimly. *It took what it could get. When Petulant Pedrock touched its hand, they both transported somewhere else.*

"But where?"

Could be anywhere in the Drowned World. Perhaps we should consider him lost forever and move on.

I smack his jar in a panic. "Jim! We can't just let him become some kind of sad, rotten witch who thinks he can raise the dead."

Shrunken Jim's mouth-stitches sag. *Fine. That other witch was a silver-tongued liar of the worst variety. Raising the dead? Pah.*

Even though I already decided the bargain was bad news, disappointment clenches my heart. "So . . . it is impossible, then?"

Ghosts are only echoes, Shrunken Jim says gently. *Whatever that witch can raise, it won't be your parents.*

I take a breath. No looking back anymore. Only forward.

I gather my senses and turn around to try to find Oliver. That turns out to be easier said than done, because I can still feel the tug of the curse somewhere nearby. My body doesn't want to start searching for something else. But I can't—I *won't*—break the curse without my brother.

It's almost impossible to tell where they've gone. The light in the cavern is honey thick and syrupy with magic as I walk back the way I came. Witches follow me from the shadows, hissing promises at me, and I have to plug my ears to keep them at bay. I end up humming Mam's old song to distract myself: *Take my hand, oh my darling; we'll outrun the dark.* Shrunken Jim joins in too: *Don't go away now; you have stolen my heart.* We hum together, over and over, blocking out the pull of the curse and the witches' words. I manage to scale a small, high outcrop of rock to scan for Oliver, but there's no sign of him. Just a near-endless space crammed with boats and bones and charms, lost things glittering and glimmering and chattering in a thousand forgotten tongues.

"Oliver!" I shout. "Ollie, where—"

My foot almost slips off the sloped edge of the outcrop. I stumble into the cave wall to keep myself from falling. But when my shoulder hits the rock, it's softer than I expected. Too soft to be rock at all. And that's when I notice something very, very unnatural.

There is a creature in the wall.

A strangled gasp escapes me as I crane my neck upward, taking it in. Gold-washed scales like the ones we found in the tunnel blend seamlessly with the rest of the cavern—except these scales are attached to a real, actual world-serpent. And it's *alive.* I can see its ginormous body moving ever so slightly, breathing in and out, even though it's basically fused with the rock. Even with my neck tipped all the way back, I can't see its head.

"Oh," I squeak. "How long has it been sleeping here?"

Shrunken Jim seems awed too. *Forever, by the looks of it. Time moves differently for the megafauna.*

Tentatively, I reach out a hand. Then I stop myself. What did Holloway say? *The Drowned World doesn't like when magic is broken or taken away. There are creatures down there that could react to the disturbance. Creatures that are dangerous enough to cause damage to Eelgrass Bog and Wick's End.* I'm starting to understand what she meant. If this giant serpent woke up, it would collapse half the Drowned World. If we plan on breaking our curse, best not to disturb the megafauna more than necessary.

I keep walking, a new nervousness settled into my bones. How many other monsters are hidden in the walls?

Sure, this place is wondrous, but every minute we're here is another minute we're in danger. *Real* danger. And worst of all I have no idea where Oliver is or what I'm doing.

I hum Mam's song louder, clambering over boulders that feel as though they're breathing too. Around a too-big whale skeleton. Through a maze of rocky pillars pockmarked with moving, swirling fossils. Soon I've passed the entrance to the bone staircase, and I find myself walking a narrow path right along the golden river's edge. The thrum of magic is so loud, I can hardly hear myself humming anymore. To keep the fright at bay, I pretend I'm searching for Oliver inside the Unnatural History Museum, that I'm bumping into display cases instead of stalagmites, and the strange hisses belong to grouchy pipes instead of witches. It almost works. Even though my brain still feels foggy, even though my heart is still banging in my throat, I manage to stay focused. I manage to remember why I'm here.

And then I spot them. My brother and the webby witch. They're backed up against a smaller cavern, hidden from the river's glow. The witch is hissing in a low voice. Oliver glances nervously around, eyes magic-glazed.

"Don't be a turnip, Ollie!" I yell, tripping over a pile of old boots as I hurry toward him. "C'mon, we need to go!"

His head jerks, startled. But he doesn't move anywhere.

Let him make his choice, the witch snarls.

"It's not worth it," I say to Oliver when I reach him, ignoring the witch. "You fought so hard to save your memories—to stay who you are. Don't give that up."

"But . . . Mam and Da . . ."

"They wouldn't want this," I pant. "We have to hold on to the happy times we already had."

Oliver looks ready to cry. "That's just it. My notes . . . the work . . . it was practical stuff, important stuff, but I couldn't remember it all. You got to keep our family photographs. And I . . . I tried, but I forgot those things. Happy things, I think. But I can't remember."

It's okay, the witch whispers. It reaches out a webbed hand again. *Stay. Let yourself forget the topside world.*

No, Shrunken Jim snaps.

I stand on my toes until I'm eye to eye with Oliver. "So

what if we're both full of holes? There's a whole future waiting for us, Ollie. If we break the curse, we can make new memories that we won't forget."

Think of your parents, the witch growls.

"Our parents are dead," I say, although it breaks my heart to speak those words aloud. "They aren't coming back."

Oliver sobs.

"I know you did your best," I continue, swallowing down a sob of my own. "With your paperwork and . . . and all that grown-up stuff they left behind. And I'm sorry I'm not the kind of sister you felt you could share that with."

"That's not . . ." Oliver looks stricken. "Kess, I—"

"We both chose the museum. But it's about time we chose each other, right? You're my brother." I swipe a wobbly hand across my runny nose. "I don't want to lose you too."

He blinks hard. Tears streak through the mud on his cheeks. But when he opens his eyes again, they're a little less glassy. A little more *him*. He takes a shuddery breath. "Good. Because I'm not going anywhere."

"No witch bargains?"

He hesitates. Then nods. "No witch bargains."

Before I can feel too relieved, the witch gives a frustrated shriek. *Ungrateful trespassers! Who do you think you are, turning down the Drowned World's gifts?*

Go! Shrunken Jim yells.

I don't need telling twice. I grab Oliver's sleeve and run—just as the witch lurches toward us with its needle-sharp teeth

bared. And even though it runs like a broken puppet, it's *fast*.
It stays right on our heels, clawed hands outstretched.

To make matters worse, running through the Drowned
World is a lot harder than walking. The rocky ground is slippery and uneven. Fear makes my legs wobbly. My boot snags
in an old fishing net hidden beneath the shadows, but I shake
it off and don't slow down.

"Kess," Oliver wheezes, tripping along beside me, "you can . . .
let go . . . of my arm. It's . . . I'm fine."

I shoot him a suspicious glare. Then I trip again and have
to let go of Oliver to prevent both of us from face-planting
into the golden river. But he doesn't turn back to the witch,
who is still only a couple of paces behind us. He just pushes
me in front of him and keeps running. I follow the magnetic
tug in my chest, imagining an invisible thread guiding our way
toward the curse. Still the witch doesn't stop chasing us. No
matter how our path zigzags, no matter how fast we run, it
sticks close on our heels, gnashing its teeth. My breath comes
in panicky gasps. What happens if it catches us?

Try to squeeze under that arch, Shrunken Jim says urgently.
You're smaller; you should—

"Duck!" Oliver yells suddenly.

He shoves me aside just as the witch lurches close enough to
swipe a webbed hand through the air, narrowly missing my ear.

Where will you go? the witch hisses. *There's no way out.*

Heart beating about a thousand times per minute, I stumble
upright. Now that we've slowed, the witch has us both within

grabbing distance. It really is terrifying. Webbed fingers with pointy nails. Teeth jutting yellow and crooked from slimy, pale lips. Eyes black from end to end. No wonder Dr. Stoat still has nightmares about witches. I've been armed with tales of the unnatural since I could walk, but fear still grips my bones. I don't want to be stuck down here forever. I don't want to become a witch. I really, really don't.

My breath wheezes—I'm struggling to get enough air in my lungs. The narrow arch Shrunken Jim pointed out is up ahead, but I'm not sure I can race the witch. I definitely can't keep running for much longer. So I gather my fierceness and scream, "Go away! Leave us alone!"

Or what? the witch growls. *What could two topside children possibly do?*

"The curse," Oliver interrupts, jaw slackening. "Kess, I think it's here. In the rocks."

An electric jolt shivers through me. He's right. Through the fear, I can feel a tug banging against my rib cage. But the witch has us cornered. I take another step backward. The witch grins.

On your left, Shrunken Jim whispers, *there is something very pointy.* I blink. "What?"

There's no time for him to answer. The witch lunges. I seize whatever pointy thing was hidden in the rock beside me. And without thinking, I swing it hard at the witch's skull. The witch shrieks and collapses into a dazed pile, inches from my feet.

Gasping, I look at the thing in my hand. I'm expecting—and hoping—to see a sword.

"A tent pole," Oliver puffs. "Cute."

"It worked, didn't it?"

Not for long, Shrunken Jim warns.

Sure enough, the witch is already stirring. I look between the honeycombed rock and Oliver, keeping the tent pole clenched in my fist just in case.

"Go on, Kess," Oliver says. He's doubled over, trying to catch his breath. "You're the expert in finding unnatural objects. I'll watch the witch. You . . ." He gestures at the rocks.

I gulp. Then I give Oliver the tent pole and set Shrunken Jim's jar on a boulder. It's here. I can feel it. It's making my insides fizz and buzz, like I'm approaching a live wire. Carefully, carefully, I crouch on my heels. I reach into a fist-sized hole inside the rock, tensed up in case I touch something alive. My palm skims across smooth stone.

And I find the curse.

As soon as I touch it, I know. It's got an angriness to it, like there's seventy years of resentment and guilt squashed inside. But there's a spark of love too. The part of the curse that was meant to protect us. The part that somehow got buried under everything else.

It isn't particularly large or grand. Just a knotted wreath made from dried reeds, shards of broken glass, a couple of delicate songbird feet, and locks of hair.

Oliver inhales sharply when I pull it free. "What now?" he asks. "How do we break it?"

Same as you break anything, Shrunken Jim says.

"Then what will happen?"

I turn the curse over in my palm. Perhaps we'll wake the

monsters in the cave walls. Perhaps we'll immediately age seventy years. We could emerge onto Eelgrass Bog grizzled and wrinkled. Or we might turn to dust right here and now. But maybe, if we break it with enough hope in our hearts, we might get to walk away and enjoy a life full of things we'll actually remember.

There's only one way to find out.

The witch stirs, hissing through its sharp teeth. It's still unconscious. For now.

Swallowing, I press the curse into Oliver's hand. My fingers stay clasped around a clump of braided reeds. "Ready?"

"No," he admits.

I try to grin. "Be brave, Ollie."

"I don't feel very brave."

"Me neither."

"But I guess *feeling* brave isn't a requirement for *being* brave." Oliver almost manages to grin back. "That's what Da would say, at least."

Very wise, Shrunken Jim snaps. *Now hurry up.*

"On three?" I say.

Oliver swallows. "One."

Two, Shrunken Jim says.

The cavern falls silent. It's like the whole Drowned World has held its breath, all the witches and monstrous things peering in to see what will happen next.

I bite my tongue. "Three," I say.

Oliver and I tug sharply.

And the curse breaks.

28

"Do you know what an endling is, Kess? Why we chose to call ourselves the Endling Society?"

"No. Oliver doesn't tell me anything."

"It means the last survivor of a species. When the endling dies, the whole species goes extinct. Can you imagine anything lonelier than being the last of your kind, knowing it's too late to save anyone? Knowing the story ends with you?"

"Like that thylacine at the zoo?"

"Exactly."

"Jules, this really isn't cheering me up."

"Don't you see? It should be impossible to have a society of endlings. But no matter how terrible things seem, no matter how much you feel like your story is ending, you aren't alone. That's what makes the Endling Society special. Not digging up monster bones or discovering underground worlds. Just . . . being alive, together. Even when it seems impossible."

I gasp and stumble over. A thousand memories wash over me in waves. Seventy years' worth of lost moments, all coming back at once. Laughter. Tears. Bonfires. Picnics. Slammed doors. Screams into pillows. Faces. Songs. Voices.

"Listen, Kess, your father and I have been asked to investigate something unnatural happening in Antarctica. It won't be long, only a few weeks, *but it's important that you and your brother look out for each other until—"*

"No," I cry. "Don't go!"

But before I can warn them, another memory hits, and *we're spinning through the reeds, round and round until the stars are fiery slashes above. We're howling, laughing, wild as the storm above, Oliver and his best friend and the strange new girl from the spider-house—*

"Kess!"

I try to open my eyes, but my lashes are gummy with dust. The ground is shaking, or maybe that's just me. And then I'm *in the Unnatural History Museum, hiding inside the woolly whale's rib cage like I always do when the world gets too scary, a candle clutched in my fist, and Oliver is trying to find me—*

"Oliver?"

"Kess!"

I find his hand and cling tight, trying to keep my head above the ocean of memories as it crashes over me. The lid of Shrunken Jim's jar bites into my other hand. But although it's overwhelming to have so many memories crash through me, it isn't *bad*. My empty places are stitching closed. I don't feel hollow anymore.

"We did it," I say breathlessly.

Oliver looks as stunned as I feel, as though swarms of memories are beating their wings inside his head too. "Are we . . . okay?"

You won't be if you don't get out of here fast, Shrunken Jim hisses. *You've disturbed the magic. The Drowned World is waking up.*

"It wasn't awake before?" I say in disbelief. But it doesn't take long to realize he's right. The air has changed. The magic has shattered and sharpened. And when I glance to where the world-serpent was asleep in the walls, my veins turn icy.

The creature is moving.

Its ginormous scaled body shifts. The ground trembles. Cracks spiderweb through the cave walls, rubble rains downward, and waves churn across the golden river. The witches must've sensed trouble too, because they have all disappeared. It's just us and the broken remains of our curse. A strange, ringing pressure starts to build like an off-key song, scraping its nails across my eardrums until I have to grit my teeth against it.

"Let's go." I gather up Shrunken Jim's jar. "If we find the bone staircase—"

I don't get the chance to finish. The ground quakes, and I trip backward into a stalagmite. It doesn't hurt. Just a bump. But my grip on Shrunken Jim's jar slips. His eyes widen. His mouth-stitches form a surprised O as he drops.

"No!" I lurch forward to catch him before he hits the ground. My fingers close around empty air. The next second seems to last a whole eternity as he falls, falls, falls.

Then comes the horrid tinkle of broken glass.

"Jim!" I scream. The pressure climbs, forcing me to crouch and cover my ears with my hands. More rubble falls, and dust blooms into the air. I reach blindly through the cloud of dust, desperately hoping I imagined the sound of glass breaking—maybe the jar only cracked?

"What's happening?" Oliver yells. I can barely hear him over the roaring and crumbling rocks.

"I dropped his jar," I wail.

"You *what?*"

"Shrunken Jim! I can't see him!"

"Well, he can't have gotten—"

Oliver's words break off into a strangled cry as a loud crack comes from above and he dives to avoid a shower of rubble from the cavern's ceiling. Terror twists my stomach. I need to get Shrunken Jim before his jar is damaged further. I need to make sure Oliver is okay. I need to find the bone staircase so we can climb out of the Drowned World. But my lungs are filling with dust, and fear makes it impossible to think. Doesn't help that my head is still swimming with memories.

"My knee," Oliver gasps. "I think—I think I've sprained it."

I swat at the air, trying to clear the dust enough to see. "Can you stand?"

"Yes. Well—ow!—kind of."

That's something, I think numbly. But we can't go anywhere without Shrunken Jim.

That's what makes the Endling Society special. It isn't too late to save each other.

Finally, finally, my fingers scrabble against glass. "Jim?"

Kess, his voice comes weakly. So weak I'm not sure I haven't imagined it.

Relief pours through me. But when I lift his jar, it's cracked so bad I can hardly see his face stitches.

It's okay, he whispers. *Kess, you have to let me out now.*

"But you need the jar to leave the Drowned World!"

This jar isn't going anywhere anymore.

"Don't be ridiculous. Look, I . . . I can carry you," I say, trying to gather the pieces into my lap. But the liquid inside is leaking everywhere. My breath skip-jumps into a sob.

It's okay, he repeats. *Anyway, you can't leave the way you came. That tunnel collapsed.*

"You can't—"

Kess, Shrunken Jim says urgently. *You've already disturbed the magic. But when you open my jar—when you release a demon like me back into the Drowned World—it's going to get much worse. I have a plan, but I need you to listen to me very, very carefully. Can you do that?*

My eyes prickle, and it isn't from the dust. "You've been my best friend, Jim."

It's been a privilege. Truly. Shrunken Jim's voice sounds thick too. *Now, do you trust me?*

I nod.

Then open the jar.

Even with my shaky hands, the lid comes off easily. There's a *pop* like a soda can opening. Then the rest of the jar crumbles away into my lap, soaking my muddy clothes with who knows what.

And the magic explodes.

Across the cavern, barely a hundred meters away, the world-serpent opens its eyes. It seems even bigger now that it's awake. Too big for words. It moves sluggishly, but every twitch sends boulder-sized rocks crashing loose. The pressure rises into a roar, so loud I'm worried my ears might burst. And with a sudden lurch, its head breaks free. The ground bucks, and I'm tossed sideways like a rag doll. Pain spreads hot across my rib cage.

"Kess!" Oliver yells. "What did you do?"

Pugnacious Pedrock. Never asking the good questions.

I look up. At first I think it's another witch, but this figure is even less human than the witches. It flickers like a guttered candle, with legs that bend the wrong way and teeth in all the wrong places. Its moss-green body stands twice as tall as an adult and reminds me of an insect, something between a toad and praying mantis. Power clings to it, thick enough to touch. I can't help but shiver. Still, I recognize those bulbous eyes and the smile that curves as wide as a waxing moon, now that it's no longer bound by stitches.

"Jimontheos," I whisper. "Demon fearsome and extraordinaire."

He scoffs sadly. *Hush up. Now, when I tell you to move, fetch your bothersome brother. Then you need to grab hold of that ridiculous snake, close your eyes, and do not let go unless your hands fall off. Actually, not even then. Understood?*

I gape. "You want me to grab the world-serpent?"

I want you to do something miraculous, Kess Pedrock. His shadow flickers as a pillar of rock comes crashing down. *I want you to live.*

"But—"

Move, Kess!

I swallow the pain from my bruised rib cage and run toward Oliver. He squawks in surprise when I catch his arm until I hiss, "It's just me, idiot." My eyes are turned downward because of all the falling dust. But I can still see the roiling body of the world-serpent smashing through the rock up ahead. With a ripple of gold, it surges across the cavern until it's almost next to us.

Shrunken Jim moves in front of us, puffed up to something nearly as big and strange as the world-serpent itself. *Overgrown worm*, he scoffs.

Then he launches himself at the serpent's mouth and vanishes in an explosion of green. Light spills over its scaly coils like a glove, the same color as the liquid in Shrunken Jim's jar. The world-serpent roars. But it sounds muffled now. The magical pressure in the air has shrunk like it's all been sucked into the green glow coating the world-serpent, same as a vacuum sucks up dust.

Grab on now! Shrunken Jim's voice comes from everywhere and nowhere. *I've contained its magic as much as I can!*

It really does sound like madness. The sensible part of me wants to run as far away from the world-serpent—and the falling rocks—as possible. That feeling only grows as the snake's body thrashes right past us, blowing back my hair with a wave of static light. Before I can think too much about it, I take a breath and run to shove my hands beneath the plate-like scales. Light zaps through me like an electric charge. Underneath, the world-serpent's body feels as cool and slippery as a regular snake—except this one is thicker than a tree trunk and almost yanks my arm from its socket when it twists. It doesn't seem to notice I'm hanging on, because it doesn't slow down at all. I grit my teeth and wrestle my body onto the serpent as though it's a horse, wrapping my legs as tight as I can.

As I'm pulled through the air, I hear Oliver yell, "You've got to be joking!" He's a pale blur, still standing on the ground beside Shrunken Jim's broken jar and our dust-covered curse.

"Ollie!" I shout. "C'mon!"

I hear him swear. Then, as the serpent slows ever so slightly, he launches himself at one of the coils behind me and grabs on for dear life.

Good, Shrunken Jim says. *Now, hold on!*

The green light brightens, so dazzling I have to close my eyes tight. The world-serpent whips and bucks, but the movements feel different now. Less angry and more . . . *afraid*. It roars in confusion, and the light grows and grows. I tuck my head against the scales and hold, hold, hold until my muscles burn.

"What's happening?" Oliver yells.

I don't get a chance to reply. The world-serpent gives one final roar . . . and charges up, up, up through the Drowned World ceiling. Oliver and I are plunged into darkness as dirt and rock and roots whip past, stinging my skin. The world-serpent goes faster, faster—

—and breaks the surface of Eelgrass Bog.

29

For a moment we're birds, soaring skyward. As the air opens from cave to sky, the magic clinging to the world-serpent breaks free and pushes the green light away in shock waves that race across Eelgrass Bog like ripples over a puddle. The ground shakes and splits. Nearby birch trees whither. Peculiar purple flowers bloom and die in the space of a blink.

Then the green light snaps back to the world-serpent's body, same as a rubber band stretched too far. Static shivers down my arms. My grip loosens. Just as the serpent unleashes a bone-quaking roar that sends nearby geese scattering in a panic, my fingers slip free from the scales. I cry out, fall into Oliver, and knock us both from the serpent's back.

We land face-first in a puddle with a *splat*.

By the time I've picked myself up and spat out a mouthful of muck, the world-serpent's head has plunged back into the ground. The rest of its gold-and-green body thrashes like lightning. I watch, stunned. Eelgrass Bog continues to shake after the world-serpent's tail disappears into a brand-new tunnel, tumbling trees and splashing puddle water over my face. And then everything goes still.

And I laugh.

"Huh? What's funny?" Oliver wobbles upright, wringing water from his clothes. He's covered head to toe with dust and dirt. A nasty scrape traces across his forehead, and his knee looks swollen. I shouldn't laugh, especially since I bet I look like a beaten-up bog mummy too. But I can't help it.

"We're alive!" I say. "We went to the Drowned World, broke the curse, and we're still alive!"

Oliver blinks. Then a smile spreads across his grubby face. And it really is *his* face, not aged seventy years or twisted by magic. There's even a pink flush behind his ordinarily paper-pale cheeks, a spark that makes him seem properly *here* instead of halfway to becoming a ghost. "Who knew?" he says. "You're actually right."

"We're alive," I repeat giddily. The words taste so delicious. The whole world feels brighter now that my brain cobwebs have been blown away. My head still prickles from the strange light, but that sensation is fading fast. I take a greedy gulp of fresh air. It's incredible how something as simple as breathing can feel magical. My bruised ribs ache as I exhale, but I can't stop grinning. Each thrum of my heart sounds like a chant: *alive, alive, alive.*

I want you to do something miraculous, Kess Pedrock.

Oliver's smile fades at my changed expression. "What's wrong?"

"Shrunken Jim. He saved us," I say, remembering the broken glass jar with a stab of sorrow. "But . . . he's gone."

Oliver gives me an awkward pat on the shoulder. "Sorry, Kess. I know he was your friend."

I nod, not trusting myself to speak. I wipe my face with my sleeve. Then I yelp and jerk my arm away. "Ouch!"

A tiny, red-tipped thorn is poking from the back of my hand. I try to brush it off, but it won't budge. Surprised, I turn my hands over and over. There are thorns sprouted across the ridges of my knuckles on both hands, growing right up through my skin—same as the brambles and feathers of the witches in the Drowned World.

"Look," I say, showing Oliver.

"Gross."

"It's not gross. It's just . . . unnatural."

"At least *I* don't . . ." He trails off, hand flying to the back of his head. With a *snap*, he yanks out a squashed white flower. His nose wrinkles. "Seriously? Daisies?"

My mouth quirks. "Were you hoping for antlers?"

"I don't know. Guess I was hoping not to change at all."

Again, I remember the Drowned World witches and how they were nearer to monster than human. How the magic made my thoughts sticky and clumped like boiled sugar. How close Oliver came to abandoning himself for the promise of our parents' ghosts.

"I don't think this counts as changing," I say, raising my hand to get a better look at the thorns. "Not in the ways that matter, anyway."

We stand quietly for a moment, watching the geese soar toward the blush-colored sunrise. Pale light spills across Eelgrass Bog. It pools across the ruined birch thickets and into the new serpent tunnel. A couple of pale shapes poke up through the churned dirt: bones. This could be the first time they've seen sunlight in a thousand years.

"Ready to go back to Wick's End?" Oliver asks.

I nod resolutely. "Let's go find a runaway house."

Eelgrass Bog is different as we walk home. Not just because of the damage the world-serpent caused when it broke through the surface either. There's something missing. Something invisible. The magical tug pulling me toward the Drowned World has disappeared, and it makes Eelgrass Bog seem more vast and empty than ever. Even the quiet is bigger without Shrunken Jim's commentary.

As we trudge across the muck, swatting at blackflies, I let my mind wander through the new memories that swim through my skull. Mam bandaging my knee after I fell off my first bike. Oliver and Da having a spaghetti-eating contest. Trying to drink milk through my nose. Silly, small moments. But the more I let myself remember, the more I start to recall more complicated things too. Like crouching in the Unnatural History Museum's hallway, listening to Mam and Da discuss money in anxious whispers. Spending weekends plucking moth eggs from taxidermy animals. Da climbing a too-tall ladder with a pail of paint, trying to disguise a crack in the ceiling. Mam in the garden, pulling weeds until she was covered with bramble scratches and bug bites.

A funny ache settles over me. These are the memories that rotted away, the ones that weren't saved by the happy photographs Oliver gave me.

I always figured the Unnatural History Museum was perfect before Mam and Da left. Except that was because I only remembered half the story. I'd forgotten the hard times in between. Running a museum was a lot of work, even with four of us. My parents exhausted themselves trying to keep everything afloat. So . . . maybe they *wouldn't* be disappointed to find the Unnatural History Museum tumbled down and tired. Maybe it was never my job to fix something that wasn't perfect to begin with.

"That's why they went to Antarctica, isn't it?" I say quietly.

Oliver's brows knit together. "Huh?"

"We were already running out of money. The Unnatural History Museum was already falling apart. That's why Mam and Da took the Antarctica job. They didn't want to, but they figured it was the only way to keep the museum."

Oliver scratches at a daisy growing from his hair, expression troubled. "Yes. The company promised to send someone to look after us, but . . ."

"Nobody came."

"No. They didn't."

So we were left alone in a museum that was broken from the start.

It makes me feel . . . strange, mostly. Mam and Da didn't abandon us without a reason. But they also put themselves in danger to save the Unnatural History Museum. I watch Oliver's gangly shadow walk beside mine, and I know—I *know*—my parents wouldn't want us to make the same mistake as them. They'd want us to save each other first. A smile pulls at my lips, and I'm surprised by how free I suddenly feel, like I've taken off a pair of iron shoes. Oliver notices and his frown deepens.

"What? What's funny?"

"Nothing. Just . . ." I kick at a grassy tussock, still smiling. *Maybe Mam and Da would be proud of me after all.* But that sounds too heavy to speak aloud, so instead I say, "You owe me a packet of chocolate buttons. I remember the ones you stole from my eleventh birthday stash."

Oliver groans. "Seriously? That was seventy-one years ago."

Seventy years. Even now, it's hard to wrap my head around. The megafauna skeletons in the Drowned World could've been thousands of years old. In the Unnatural History Museum, we've got fossils older than mountains. The mud we're sloshing through right now is probably crawling with ancient stuff that watched oceans grow and die over Eelgrass Bog—compared to that, seventy years is only a blink. But it's a very long time to be alone. I can feel those empty hours sitting heavy in my bones. The endless days spent doing chores in the Unnatural History Museum, ticking along like a broken clock. No wonder remembering made Oliver sick. Memories are a lot for a person to carry, and we've got enough to cover a lifetime.

"All right," I say graciously. "Clean slate. I'll forgive you for the chocolate."

"Good. I only stole them because *you* stole my underwear and hung it from the woolly whale skeleton." Oliver sighs. "You were a pain."

"But you love me."

Oliver sighs again, louder. He doesn't tell me I'm wrong.

I keep shuffling through my new memories like a deck of cards as we approach Wick's End. There's no sign of Holloway's house on the way. However, as the watch fires come into view, I notice something is wrong here too. Smoke billows wilder than usual. The air is acrid, like burned rubber tires. Then I hear the shouts.

"What the . . . ?" Oliver fumbles for his glasses. The wire rims are bent awfully out of shape, but he jams them over his nose just the same. "Oh, vermin."

I squint. "What's wrong?"

Oliver is already running. I run after him, each step making a *sluuurp* noise in the mud. It doesn't take very long to see what the problem is.

The watch fires have grown.

Flames reach twice as far as usual, burning up grass and peat that should have been safely out of reach. Normally the firepits are large enough to stop the flames from spreading, and as far as I know, the watch fires have never *tried* to grow before. But something must've made them flare unnaturally wide—almost like something very, very unnatural passed through. A spark must've caught the nearby grass. Now it looks like the two watch fires are racing toward each other.

Fire trucks have already arrived, although they've been forced to park far away on account of the mud. People run back and forth with hoses and buckets of water. They hardly glance twice at me and Oliver as we cross into Wick's End, and this time, the watch fires barely flicker when we pass. Just a little cough. Just enough to remind me of the thorns pricking through my knuckles.

"What happened?" I ask as a firefighter runs past.

She turns to me in surprise. "Kids, you shouldn't be here."

"Was it the . . . earthquake?"

The firefighter barks a laugh. "Have you ever seen an earthquake spark a fire in a bog before? Unless you listen to the folks who saw a *house* run through the watch fires and–"

"Svenson! Hurry up!" another firefighter shouts.

As she sprints off toward the blaze, Oliver and I share a worried look.

The town is a smoke-thick disaster zone. Even with Shrunken Jim's light holding back the world-serpent's power, some of the magical shock waves must've reached town. Windows have shattered. Cars have rolled into each other. Fences are toppled. Sirens and alarms shriek like the world's worst orchestra, though, luckily, nobody seems to be hurt. It's mostly the older buildings that are damaged, the ones with creaky wooden walls like–

"The Unnatural History Museum," I gasp.

We round a corner, and my fears come true.

The Unnatural History Museum is in pieces. And it's pretty clear what's responsible for most of the damage.

Holloway's house has crashed into the museum's side.

Where the entrance hall used to be, there's now a jumble of stilts, timbers, and torn-down ivy. It's impossible to tell where Holloway's house ends and the museum begins. Here and there, I can make out display cases and broken exhibits—parts of skeletons, a kraken tentacle, a were-walrus tusk—mixed with Holloway's books and broken tea jars.

"Oh," I say. It's all I can manage.

"Kess! Kess, over here!"

A figure hops through the rubble with a messy black braid and messier pajamas. Moments later, a second figure follows. Holloway's heavy green coat is powdered with dust, and she looks absolutely furious, but when she notices us, relief passes across her face.

"You're alive," she whispers, as though hardly daring to believe it.

I'm about to reply when Lilou barrels into me, almost knocking us both into the splintered wreck of our old front door.

"I can't believe it! Geez, I've been so nervous I could puke," she says breathlessly. "Did you see the Drowned World? Is the curse broken? Are you okay?"

"Yes!" I laugh. "And yes, and yes."

Her hand brushes my thorns as she steps away to smile at me properly. I tense up, waiting for her to react with disgust. But she just smiles brighter. "I knew you could do it, Kess Pedrock."

"Not to interrupt," Oliver says shrilly, "but, um, have you noticed the state of our museum?"

Lilou flinches. "It—"

"Has a giant hole in it?" Holloway cuts in. The anger is back. "Whose fault might that be, Starling?"

"Um, mine." Lilou hangs her head. "One of the levers for Holloway's house broke, and, well, we sort of lost control. *I* lost control. The watch fires went wild. I wanted to leave the house on Eelgrass Bog, but I couldn't get it to stop, and your museum . . ."

My museum. The Unnatural History Museum isn't totally wrecked, but this isn't something a bucket of paint or a feather duster can fix. Newspapers from the half-squashed library blow across the street like paper birds. I take in the damage, waiting for the horror to hit me. Except it doesn't come. Of course it's sad to see my home in pieces. But the heart-soaring lightness I've felt since leaving the Drowned World doesn't vanish or dim.

"It's okay. We'll be okay," I say. And as soon as I've spoken the words aloud, I know they're true.

"What are we supposed to do now?" Oliver demands. He's gathered up several wayward newspapers and stuffed them under his armpit, almost out of habit, as though he still needs them to remember. "Our house is wrecked!"

"That makes two of us," Holloway mutters.

I'm not sure what we're supposed to do either. It's too late to save the Unnatural History Museum, just like it's too late to tell my parents not to go to Antarctica, to explain that I would choose them over the museum every single day. But it's not too late for us.

Buildings can be rebuilt. People can't.

"We'll figure it out," I say determinedly. "We're the Endling Society, aren't we? We'll find a way."

"Kess is right." Lilou takes my hand and sets her jaw. "I—I don't know how I'll explain it to my dads yet, but you can stay with us until everything is put right. Holloway included."

Holloway looks surprised. Her anger softens into something closer to weariness. "I can't stay here. Wick's End is no place for me."

"Why not?" I argue. Who says Wick's End can't be a place for people like us? Lilou didn't let go of my hand when her thumb touched the thorns on my knucklebones again. She didn't react at all, like a pinch of unnaturalness made no difference in the world.

Holloway and Oliver share a glance. I wait for Oliver to announce that he can't live with a witch. Or for Holloway to decide she can't live with a bunch of untrustworthy humans. But I guess most of us are somewhere in between witch and human anyway; and to my delight, they both nod. Holloway actually *smiles*.

"Why not?" she echoes.

We stand together and look at the wreck. Tumbled-over display cases. Rafters exposed like a crow-picked rib cage. Twisted iron stilt-legs from Holloway's house. It reminds me of a puzzle box dumped upside down, but already, I'm imagining how we can put the pieces together again. It won't have to be perfect. It won't have to be the same as my parents' museum. It won't have to attract masses of visitors. It'll be for *us*, and that'll be enough.

"This doesn't mean you're forgiven for commandeering my house and scurrying away to the Drowned World," Holloway adds.

Oliver shrugs. "Or we could call it even. You did curse us for seventy years."

"Well, then. For what it's worth . . ." Holloway holds out a clawed hand. "To the new Endling Society."

"To the Endling Society," I say immediately, shaking her hand.

Lilou grins and adds her hand to the pile. "To the Endling Society."

After a moment, Oliver lets go of his newspapers. They swirl around us with the dust and dead leaves. "To the Endling Society," he agrees.

30

F our months later and nobody agrees on what caused the earthquake.

The *official* explanation is natural causes. Of course, that didn't stop plenty of people from swearing they saw unusual things happen across Wick's End that day. Some saw a house with stilt-legs charge through town. Some saw the watch fires flare so red and high, they looked like erupting volcanoes. And some saw a peculiar green light ripple across Eelgrass Bog, charged with an electricity that made all their hairs stand on end. A kid swore it made their dog fly, just for a second.

Whispers grew into rumors. The rumors grew louder.

With the curse gone and words like "unnatural" tossed around to describe the quake, people seemed to remember that the Unnatural History Museum existed. They figured we'd have answers they couldn't find anywhere else. Our first visitors came knocking before we even had a door fixed for them to knock on.

Of course, patching up the museum was no small job. It took almost a week just to clear away the debris of Holloway's house. Plenty of exhibits were damaged. And that wasn't counting the decades of decay that had settled into the museum's bones.

But caring for the Unnatural History Museum was different from before. We weren't trying to make it into the same grand building it had been in its prime. Even my parents had struggled with that. Before anything else, we just needed a home—and we knew we couldn't do it alone.

It was Lilou's dads who came to our rescue. Lilou gave them a story filled with careful half-truths that made it seem as though we'd lost our parents very recently. To me, it barely felt like a lie. Holloway was introduced as a distant cousin come to take care of us. Luckily, Lilou is a convincing storyteller, and even with the gaps, her dads accepted her tale. Soon they were calling in favors and ringing up tradespeople. Little by little, the holes in the museum began to close. They even helped set up the Boglands Unnatural Research Preservation Society to allow interested people to become involved with the restoration. It meant the museum wasn't only ours anymore—but neither was the responsibility of looking after it.

Change hasn't been easy. But as I hurry downstairs this morning, I'm full of pride for how far we've come. The woolly whale skeleton hangs on brand-new cables. The repaired floorboards don't creak underfoot, and my parents beam down at me from their framed photographs on the wall. They'd be proud, I think. Sure, we've rebuilt smaller with far fewer exhibits. But we pulled through pretty good in the end.

"Morning, Mam and Da," I say, blowing a kiss to their special plaque. CELEBRATING HUGH AND ELLEN-JANE PEDROCK, it reads.

FOREVER IN OUR MEMORIES. We're going to create a special exhibit called *Science & Secrets: Exploring Eelgrass Bog* for our grand reopening next month. Oliver is sorting through our parents' research so we can have a section about their accomplishments. We've had to tweak some dates, of course. But after so long in the dark, I'm glad we finally get to share them—to *talk* about them—along with the rest of the Unnatural History Museum. We've even had assistance from another actual scientist. Turns out Holloway wasn't the only person to move from Eelgrass Bog to Wick's End after the quake affected the watch fires.

"Kid," Dr. Stoat says in greeting as he emerges from the library. He's swapped his bulky leather coat for an orange raincoat that spills down to his knees, making him look kind of like a grouchy traffic cone. But he fits here. His *work* fits here. The Unnatural History Museum seems to be helping him look forward instead of backward—it probably helps to be around people who understand what it means to be touched by unnatural magic. Holloway says Dr. Stoat is a difficult case because he was never cursed, which means there's no easy way to break the Drowned World's hold over him. Sometimes he still stares into space. Sometimes he still panics that witches are coming for him. All we can do is be patient and believe in him. Maybe it sounds silly, but I reckon that's the most powerful healing tool of all: people who believe in you.

Oliver comes out of the library moments later with an armful of notebooks. He hasn't dropped his habit of writing everything down, like he's afraid his memories might lose their stickiness and vanish one day.

"You're up late," he tells me.

"It's a weekend! And it's only..." I check a nearby clock and wince. Guess I am running late. Sleep has been tricky since we broke the curse; Dr. Stoat was right about the nightmares. They aren't *bad* bad. But every now and then, I wake up with a gold light burning behind my eyes and visions of cursed creatures about to snatch my heart away.

Dr. Stoat looks at me and grunts, as though he's read my mind. Then he shuffles off down the corridor.

"I made treacle porridge if you're hungry. There's a pot in the kitchen," Oliver says. "Well. Unless Ivy ate it."

"What's this about Ivy?" Holloway pokes her head through a curtain of plastic that's blocking off the almost complete Skeleton Gallery. She's been working on a "surprise" that I'm 99 percent certain is her golden stag, since I can see it taking shape through the curtain. "Oh, hello, Kess. Make sure you stay away from the kitchen today. There's something evil in the pot pretending to be porridge."

Oliver scowls and tugs at a dandelion growing behind his ear.

I just roll my eyes. Oliver and Holloway enjoy acting as though they despise each other, but there's no bite behind their words anymore. Especially when they think nobody is looking, they're ... well, happy. Relaxed. The loneliness Holloway used to wear beneath her skin has faded away, and I've caught her awkwardly speaking to the Starlings when they visit. Even Dr. Stoat has stopped grumbling about Holloway being a *good-for-nothing witch*. Mostly. And whenever we hold an Endling Society meeting (usually just to drink fancy tea and eat grilled cheese sandwiches) we can pass hours together without a single mean comment. I know it'll take time for the ghosts of the old Endling Society to die completely. Maybe they never will. But I reckon the best families aren't perfect anyway.

"'S okay," I say. "We're making pancakes at Madeline's house."

"In that case, you better hurry up before Miss Starling comes looking for you." Holloway sighs. "Last time she almost broke the doorbell."

I hug them both, bursting with heart-glow when Oliver *and* Holloway hug me back. "Enjoy your belching club!" I call as I toe on a pair of sneakers.

They groan.

"Get a new joke," Oliver grumbles. Really, he should've thought about that before he named the Boglands Unnatural Research Preservation Society. He said it sounded very official and grown-up. It does, kind of. But it also spells out BURPS. It's even embroidered onto their shirt pockets: PROUD BURPS MEMBER.

When I step outside, I almost bump into Lilou, who's coming down the pathway in the opposite direction.

"Kess!" She beams. "About time."

"Sorry. Forgot to set my alarm," I say sheepishly. "You, um, look pretty today."

And she really does. Honeyed sunlight falls across her shiny black braids, and her cheeks dimple as she smiles wider. "Flatterer," she says. Then she leans in, and her lips brush mine. It's only a whisper, only a second, but an electric zap jolts all the way down to my toes. My stomach explodes into butterflies. We haven't had a proper conversation about *like*-liking each other since that night on Eelgrass Bog. I'd tumble it up if I tried. But not everything needs to be labeled, sorted, and displayed like a museum exhibit. One day I'll work up the courage to tell Lilou exactly how I feel, but for now, I think we understand each other just fine.

Hand in hand, we walk down the pathway. Around the winding streets of Wick's End, past the Mulberry Tree and the schoolyard, all the way to the edge of Eelgrass Bog. It's the roundabout route to Madeline's house, but after the earthquake, everyone agrees that Eelgrass Bog is the place to be if you want to catch a glimpse of the unnatural.

It looks different now that the watch fires have grown. New pits were created to stop the flames from spreading farther. They don't form a neat parallel line anymore. The border between Eelgrass and Wick's End has gone . . . wonky. New footpaths push farther into the bog, far enough that I notice dog walkers through the distant birch thickets. And if I squint, sometimes I can make out a strange shape in the no-man's-land between Wick's End and Eelgrass Bog. A greenish figure with too-long limbs, teeth everywhere, and bulbous eyes.

As it turns out, powerful demons *can* leave the Drowned World for a short amount of time, if they want to badly enough.

I search for him today. And there he is.

The corners of his mouth tug upward. I can't hear him outside the Drowned World anymore, now that my curse has broken. But I can imagine his voice in my head just the same: *Hello, Kess.*

"Hello, Jim," I whisper back.

"Is it him?" Lilou asks, following my gaze.

I nod. My chest aches for my old friend and the stories we used to share. At least I get to see him from time to time. And no matter what, I'll get to keep the memories we shared for the rest of my life.

Across town, a clock chimes. We really are late today. A group of us who are starting seventh grade at Wick's End Middle School next year are meeting to make costumes for the end-of-year formal in a few weeks—and to eat pancakes, of course. I am nervous about rejoining school after so long locked away in the museum, especially when part of me will stay unnatural forever—like the thorns hidden beneath my knitted gloves. But Madeline, Sumi, Amelia, and the others are very friendly. In fact, I think we *are* friends now.

I hitch my backpack into place and tell Lilou, "Last one there is a prune-bottomed dung beetle!"

Lilou laughs. "In your dreams, Kess Pedrock!"

I'm already running. My shoes squelch into the muck as I run faster, faster, wind from Eelgrass Bog knotting my hair into tangled snarls. I don't have to look back to know Lilou and Shrunken Jim are running with me. Our shadows streak across the ground like wild things, like birds or monsters, and my heart glows, because whatever happens next, I am not alone.

ACKNOWLEDGMENTS

My sincerest thanks to my agent, Kelly Sonnack, for supporting my career with extraordinary tenacity, wisdom, and kindness. I will forever be grateful that you glimpsed the hearts of the stories I was trying to tell and made them shine with your razor-sharp editorial eye; I couldn't ask for a better partner and advocate. Thank you also to Analía Cabello, Adefisayo Adeyeye, and the entirety of the Andrea Brown Literary Agency. Maybe I'm biased, but you're all the best in the industry.

To my superstar editor, Gretchen Durning, thank you for embracing my weird little bog book and pushing Kess's story in all the right directions. Your enthusiasm and insight is unparalleled, and I feel like the luckiest author in the world to have an editor who gets exactly what I'm trying to do—perhaps better than I do!

It's a huge privilege to be working with everyone at Razorbill/Penguin Young Readers: Alex Campbell (interior designer), Brian Luster (copyeditor), Sarah Jospitre (proofreader), Misha Kydd (production editor), Jayne Ziemba (managing editor), as well as the brilliant marketing and publicity teams. I haven't stopped staring at my cover since it first landed in my inbox, so a megafauna-sized thank-you to cover designer Kaitlin Yang and artist James Firnhaber for capturing Kess (and Shrunken Jim!) in such a gorgeous, striking way.

I am eternally indebted to the Author Mentor Match program, particularly to my mentor, Heather Kassner, who believed in me first. My path would look very different without this community of generous writers. Thank you to my own mentees, Bailey, Jessie, Zubin, and Siana, for not only writing some of my very favorite middle grade manuscripts of all time, but for allowing me to share in your journeys. You are all endlessly talented.

I owe much to my academic homes over the years. Thank you to my creative writing workshop leaders at the University of Victoria, who helped teach me what it meant to write: D. W. Wilson, Mallory Tater, Bill Gaston, Yasuko Thanh. Special thanks to Karen Rivers, who read an unrecognizably early draft of this story in her undergraduate class and encouraged me to stick with it. I am fortunate to have benefited from the creative and academic communities at Lucy Cavendish College, Cambridge, especially during the depths of the pandemic. Though my journey at Queen's University is only just beginning, I am already grateful for the English faculty here and my wonderful PhD cohort.

Of course, Kess was correct about the power of hands to hold in the dark. Throughout this wild and disarming process, I've been so fortunate to cross paths with precisely the right people at the right times. Huge hugs to my support groups, including my submission solidarity people, fellow '24 debut children, and AMM MG squad. You're all brilliant sparks of light. Bigger groups I owe hugs to include the 2024 debuts, student writers, submission slog comrades, and the middle grade community at large. Thank you to Candace and Stacie for your encouragement. Thank you to Tana, Justine, Conner, Jessica, Christie, Karina, and Anastasia for lending your eyes and ears and wisdom during the earliest stages. Gratitude to Rachel and Melissa for keeping me on track when I needed it. And Riley, thank you for being here with me, and simply for being you.

Lastly and most of all, thank you to my family. Your support and encouragement means the universe to me, and writing these acknowledgments, I've never been more aware of how words sometimes aren't enough. Mum, Dad, Taz, and Clara: I love you all so very much.